By Sherry D. Ficklin

*What if the one thing you never meant to hold on to,
was the one thing you couldn't let go of?*

Losing Logan
Copyright © 2014 by: Sherry D. Ficklin

Clean Teen Publishing
PO Box 561326
The Colony, TX 75056

www.cleanteenpublishing.com

Typography by: Courtney Nuckels
Cover design by: Marya Heiman

ISBN: 978-1-940534-41-1

Dedication:
For everyone who was ever mean to me in High School.
Suck it.

Content Disclosure

For more information about our content disclosure, please utilize the QR code above with your smart phone or visit us at www.cleanteenpublishing.com.

We must never forget the people we love,
The ones who give us reason.
They come and go throughout our lives,
Like the change of every season.
Love is truly a foreign thing,
We'll never really understand.
What we think will be forever,
Is just an empty hand.
People leave you lonely,
Hurting you and your pride.
They say that they will love you,
Then shove you to the side.
Out of seven billion people,
Search for the one that's right.
To help you through your tragedies,
And fill your world with light.
One day you'll find that person,
And they will love you so.
But until that wonderful time arrives,
You must learn to let others go.

~Lexi Shaffer 2014

One

S O WHAT IF LOGAN WAS DEAD? I mean, it's not like he owed me money or anything. I pause at the top of the stairs, letting my mom move around me and walk inside. To my left a group of girls are holding each other and ugly crying. I try to assure myself that the display is genuine and has nothing to do with the swarm of reporters behind me, their cameras clicking like insects.

"I bet not one of those girls even knew Logan," I grumble.

"Firstly, everyone knew Logan. And secondly, quit being such a judgy-Mc judge-sickle."

To my right, Carlos holds out his hand, which I take and allow him to lead me inside and down the hall. Leaning over he whispers in my ear.

"I can't believe you wore that."

I look down at my dark jeans, carefully tucked into tall brown boots. My steel grey scarf hangs over my light tan sweater. I'd even taken the time to throw my long brown hair into a messy bun.

"We can't all afford to look like movie stars," I mumble back.

Carlos, with his rich brown skin and dark hair looks like he should be on a billboard somewhere, and the dark fitted suit he's wearing only enhances the effect. He's gorgeous. One of those genetically gifted boys who could bat his eyelashes and have any girl he wanted. You know, if he actually wanted girls. He weaves our arms together and pulls me up to a tall pedestal with an open book laying on it. A few people in front of us are signing in like they are registering for a giveaway at the mall. I shift uncomfortably.

"Relax, Zoe. It isn't a funeral. Just a viewing."

I shake my head, "That's even worse." I lower my voice so no one else can hear, "Who would want to look at a dead body? I mean, it's just kinda twisted, right?"

He pats my hand. "Closure, darling. It's a chance to say goodbye."

"I said goodbye to Logan a long time ago," I say while looking ahead at the room beyond the pedestal. Rows of neatly assembled chairs are nearly filled with people from our quiet little town. Some are talking, most crying. A few are just texting or playing on their phones. I feel my breathing pick up as a warmth spreads under my skin and wraps tightly around my chest. I shudder and it slices down my spine like electricity.

"You guys were friends, right?"

I feel the frown on my face. Friends. Yeah, right.

"Our parents were friends when we were little," I say dismissively. The truth is, once we hit middle school, everything had changed between us. He got popular, and I got weird. We went our separate ways and never spoke again. Here we are, getting ready to start our senior year, and Logan would have been the reigning king of the school. I, however, am doomed to spending another year eating lunch in the drama department with Carlos while he updates his vlog, watching the school lacrosse games from under the bleachers, and spending my Friday nights reading in my bedroom. Not that there's anything wrong with any of that. A shove from behind pushes me into the group in front of me. Kaylee Greely brushes past us. She and her entourage of well dressed clones don't bother to wait in line, they go straight to the front and the crowd parts for them. Scribbling quickly like she's signing an autograph she strides into the main viewing room, not even bothering to remove her large sunglasses as she takes a seat in the front row. As Logan's girlfriend, I feel a genuine twinge of sympathy for her. Right up until she pulls out her compact and reapplies her lip gloss with a loud smack of her lips.

Carlos tilts his head and sighs deeply. For a split second I think he's admiring her ass, then I realize his eyes are laser fixed on her designer handbag and I chuckle out loud. Everyone in line turns to stare at me. I can actually feel the blood rush into my face. Carlos turns, blocking me from view and I can breathe again. He fiddles with my scarf, twisting it and tucking it until it's sitting perfectly against my small chest.

"I really don't want to do this."

Carlos tugs on my earlobe. "Don't worry Zoe Bowie, I'm here."

I shake my head. "Let me rephrase. I'm *not* doing this. I don't even like half of these people. Hell, I didn't like Logan when he was alive, and I'm not going to sit here and pretend like I miss him now that he's gone." I swallow. Imagining myself sitting in one of those black folding chairs, listening to crying girl after crying girl get up there and whine about what a great person he was and how he changed their lives. I throw up a little just thinking about it. "If my mom asks where I went, tell her I had a nervous breakdown and had to go home."

He smiles deviously. "I'll tell her that you, being the delicate flower you are, were overcome with grief and had to excuse yourself to the fainting couch," He says in a thick southern accent.

"Why thank you Miss Scarlett."

I can't help but grin. I know it's been his dream to play the lead in the local theater company's production of *Gone with the Wind* since he was five. My remark earns me a kissy face and a wave as he turns to go inside.

I'm all ready to make a break for it, when I get a glimpse of something out the corner of my eye. As I turn to get a better look, I see a boy walking away and into the coat closet at the other end of the hall. I don't know why I follow him, but my feet are moving before I can fully rationalize it to myself. My boot heels clack on the stone tile floors and sounding like a heartbeat, slow and steady. I run my fingertips along the beige walls as I pass by what I hope is the casket showroom and not some sort of demented waiting room for whoever's next in line for viewing, then a room full of comfy looking floral chairs, and finally an office. At the very end of the hall, the door to the coat room is ajar. As I reach out and push it open, an army of shivers march up my back.

If this was a horror movie, this is the part where I would die.

As soon as I step inside the door, the boy turns and my heart sinks into my feet. For a minute, I just stand there, staring at him like an idiot. All I can feel is icy cold air from the vent in the ceiling blowing down on me, chilling me to my core. Then the anger flows in, replacing the cold shock with a flush of heat. I reach behind me and slam the door shut.

"What is your freaking *damage*, Logan?"

He stares at me, his green eyes wide. "Excuse me?"

My eyes narrow. I know what's going on here. "I'm being punked, aren't I? This is some stupid reality TV show or something right?"

He just stands there looking confused.

"Does your family know you're alive? I mean, seriously, if this is some dumb publicity stunt for the reporters out front..." I'm so angry I don't even know what to say. Logan has always been a bit of an attention whore, but this is a new low. My hands are balled onto fists at my hips. "Say something, Logan. *Please.* Find the magic words to make this whole mess not be the most horrible thing a human being has ever done in their entire life, ever."

"Zoe?" his voice is soft and he has a dumb half grin on his face that I remember from when we were kids. I have a desperate urge to remove it with my fist. "What are you talking about?"

Oh, sure. Like I'm the crazy one. "You are a giant douche hammer, you know that? I mean, what is this? Some idiotic attempt to get extra credit in English class? Tom Sawyer 101? I mean, those people think you're dead! We all thought…" I trail off again, the words jumbling in my brain before I can get them out. I'm so angry I'm bordering on incoherent. My pulse is racing and my whole face feels hot. I need to calm myself before I completely lose it. I take a deep breath, hold it for a second, and then release it slowly.

He takes a step toward me, tilting his head curiously. "You can see me?"

"Okay, that's it. I'm not falling for this…whatever this is. I'm going to march in there and tell your mother right now."

He straightens, a cocky grin spreading across his face. That's a look I'm more used to seeing on him recently. "You're going to go tell my mommy on me? What, are we five again?"

I grunt and flip him off, throwing the door open.

"Wait!" I hear him call behind me but I keep going. Inside the main room his parents have taken seats next to

Kaylee in the front row. Ignoring the minister speaking from the pulpit I stride up the center aisle, stomping angrily. I'm almost to the front when I realize something. The dark brown casket is open. My pace slows and I see Logan's face, his eyes are closed like he's sleeping inside the white satin lined box. I spin, looking behind me, but he's gone. I spin back around and take the final steps to the coffin, clutching the sides for support.

Up close, I'm not sure what I'm seeing. He looks kinda puffy and waxy. Maybe that's how he's doing it. Maybe it's some kind of wax dummy. I reach out to touch his face when a sob from behind me snaps me out of it. Two pairs of arms grab me from either side, Carlos on my left and my mother on my right. They quickly usher me back down the aisle to a chorus of sobs and camera snaps. I'm shaking. Around me there is a thick white fog clouding the very edges of my vision.

"Mom?" I ask.

She's soothing me, patting my hair and rubbing my back. Outside they lead me to the car amidst more cameras clicking. I can barely walk. My knees are like Jell-O and I feel like I'm breathing through a straw. I gasp and the fog gets worse. I feel Carlos slip me into the passenger seat of mom's old Camry then he thrusts a bottle of cold, sweaty water in my hand.

"Are you okay Zoe?" My mother asks, kneeling in front of me.

She has her nurse face on and I know if I say the wrong thing, I'm going to end up spending the night in the hospital.

"I think she's in shock," Carlos says, patting my hand gently. I pull it away.

"Not helping, Carlos." I look over at my mother who is clearly on the edge of panic. "I'm fine. Just, overwhelmed. Can we just go home?" She nods, patting my knee before moving to the other side of the car. Carlos gently turns me in my seat, trying to help me buckle. Behind him, on the steps to the funeral home, Logan is standing in the sunlight. Only, the reporters are all ignoring him.

I grab Carlos by the lapel and jerk my head towards the stairs.

"Do you see that?"

He turns and looks over his shoulder. "What?"

"Do you see anyone on the steps?"

He frowns, "No. Why?"

I shake my head, squeezing my eyes shut. "Never mind. I think my breakfast grape juice fermented. I'm gonna go home and lay down for a bit."

He shuts the door and I lean out the window to give him a peck on the cheek.

"Take care, sweetie. Call me later when you are feeling better."

I tug my hair out of the bun and let it fall around my shoulders. A familiar ache is growing inside my skull and I know if I leave it in, it'll only make it worse. "I will."

He steps back onto the curb and we speed off. I don't open my eyes all the way home, I just let the cool wind blow knots into my hair and try not to think of the thousands of pictures of me freaking out coffin-side that are hitting the web as we speak, or of Logan's face in that coffin.

I fail on both counts.

By the time I open my eyes, the sun is shining full strength through my bedroom window. Somehow I've made it out of my clothes and into my soft blue pajama pants and grey tank top. I groan, rolling over and glancing at the alarm clock. The flashing red 4:13 makes me jerk up, tossing off the warm green comforter and leaping to my feet. I open my door, but the house is completely silent. A piece of paper is taped to my door.

Zoe–
Working a double shift. Call me if you aren't feeling better
soon. Don't forget to pick up what you need for school!
Love,
Mom

I rip the paper off the door and wad it into a ball, tossing it over my shoulder as I step into the hallway. The first day of school is in less than a week, but I almost can't bring myself to think of it. It's not that I hate school, per-se, but it's tedious and boring. Not even my advanced classes really challenge me, and let's face it, I'm probably going to spend the bulk of the year in the library anyway—which I'd rather do without a bunch of other people annoying me. I'm supposed to be there tomorrow since I volunteered to help set up for back to school night, but I'm actually debating blowing it off.

Then a pang of guilt sets in and I think better of it.

Mrs. Jackson had been kind enough to let me spend most of my summer there, helping out at times, or just devouring the new books. As I'm rummaging through nearly barren cabinets my cell rings on the counter. *Putting on the Ritz*, Carlos's ring tone, echoes through the house. I snatch it up.

"Hey Carlos. What's up?"

"Not much. How are you feeling? I called earlier but your mom answered. She said you were still sleeping."

I stifle a yawn. "Yeah. Sorry about that. I don't know what happened. Panic attack or something?"

Yesterday's events seem so surreal, I can't make sense of any of it. I suppose grief does weird things to the body.

"As long as you are feeling better now." His voice is hesitant, like he's waiting to gauge my reaction.

I cringe and drop the bag of Cheetos I'm holding as I remember my scene at the viewing.

"Oh shit. How bad is it?"

There is a short pause at the other end of the line. "Not terrible. Though you started quite a trend. About 30 girls threw themselves on the coffin and wept like idiots after you left."

I sigh as relief settles into my chest, releasing the tension. "Well, I suppose that's good at least. Better to be considered an attention whore than a lunatic, right? Any viral videos yet?"

"A few of the other girls posted pics, but none of you."

I frown and switch the phone to my other ear.

"I can hear you frowning, Zoe."

Now I grin. He knows me so well.

"Would you really rather be a crazy, attention grabbing, wannabe?"

I pull open the bag and stuff a cheesy poof in my mouth, crunching on it as I answer.

"Better than being invisible. I could strip naked and ride a horse down the hall in Lady Godiva style and no one would even notice."

I can hear him laughing. "Oh, honey, you don't have the figure for nudity."

I roll my eyes. "Thanks for that."

"Well, if you're quite done with the pity party, I could use some help picking out my back to school wardrobe. I'm driving to the city to hit Bloomies. Wanna join?"

"When are you going to get over your crush on the hot guy at the Bloomingdales counter?"

He huffs, "When he quits looking so good in a pair of slacks. Come on, don't crap out on me. If I go alone he will think I'm stalking him."

"You are stalking him," I say around another Cheeto.

"Well, yeah, but I don't want him to *know* that I'm stalking him."

I shake my head and take my bag of powered cheese awesomeness back to my room. "Sorry. You'll just have to go with your plastic."

"Fine. I will let my credit card be my guide. But you owe me one."

"Put it on my tab," I say, unable to keep the smile off my face as I end the call.

Brimstone, my lean black kitty, leaps onto my desk and demands affection the way only cats can.

"Well, Brim. We both knew this day was coming. Today is the day I stay in my pajamas and do nothing but glut myself on Cheetos and read books." I say it as if it's the first time that it's ever happened rather than being a semi-regular occurrence.

She rubs her head against me, unimpressed by my slothful declaration. I grab my dog-eared copy of *The Collected Works of Edgar Allen Poe* and settle in. It's a bit darker than what I've been reading lately, but it's by far one of my favorites. As I curl into my comfy old reading chair, Brim leaps up and curls into a ball on my lap. Soon I'm lost in the pages. I don't look up again until a clap of thunder shakes the house. Carefully moving Brim onto my bed I pull back my sheer curtains. The sky is dark and droplets of rain cover the glass.

I glance at the clock. It's almost seven now and

my stomach growls, taking advantage of the break in my reading to remind me that one can't live on Cheetos alone. Setting my book beside the still sleeping cat I head back to the kitchen. The kitchen light flickers but manages to stay on. I grab the long black flashlight from the junk drawer, just in case. A flash of light bursts through the windows over the kitchen sink followed quickly by a roll of thunder so loud that the tiny hairs on the back of my neck jump to attention. I shiver and pour myself a glass of milk and toss a few slices of leftover pineapple pizza onto a plate. As I turn back to my room, the lights flicker again. When the flickering stops I'm no longer alone in the kitchen. I don't scream. I think I'm too startled for that. I can't even draw in a breath. I'm frozen, unable to think beyond the face staring back at me. The glass and plate slip through my fingers, crashing to the floor and shattering at my bare feet. Logan stands in front of me with his hands held out .

"Don't move," he says urgently.

Then I scream.

Two

THE SCREAM RIPS ITS WAY UP MY BODY and explodes like a volcano out my mouth. I take a step back and feel bits of glass cut into the bottom of my foot. Lifting my weight off the foot I tumble backwards, landing in a pile of glass and porcelain.

"Stop moving," Logan commands. "You're going to cut yourself to shreds."

I take a deep breath and scream again, only this time my voice is strained so the sound comes out ragged and strangled.

"Will you please stop screaming? Seriously Zoe."

My eyes are wide. My heart is pounding against my ribcage so hard I think I might actually throw up. I take another breath, but this time I hold it in until I can't anymore and it expels in a hot rush.

"What are you doing here?"

He folds his arms, looking smug. "What am I doing here, as in here in your kitchen, or do you mean here in more general terms? As in why am I not—"

"Rotting in the ground somewhere?"

He wrinkles his nose. "I was going to say dead, but thanks for the vivid."

Slowly my senses start coming back into focus. The pain in my foot is intense, but not enough to distract from the sliver of glass stuck in my forearm.

"I'm bleeding," I say, watching the crimson leaking down my arm and off of my elbow as I inspect it.

"That happens when you fall into a pile of broken glass."

I glare at him, "Shut up, Logan."

I grab the sliver of glass with two fingers and pull it out quickly. The blood flows more freely, pooling beside me. I toss the toothpick sized sliver aside. Using my other arm like a mop to clear a space, I slide myself back out of the glass and press my back against the wall. Bringing my foot up for inspection, I see the cut. It's shallow and there is nothing in the wound. My hands shake as I pull myself to my feet, using the handle of the fridge door for support. I skirt around the glass, stepping carefully as I maneuver around Logan without looking up at him, and make my way, limping, to the bathroom.

Scooping the first aid kit from under the sink I flip the lid down and sit on the toilet. I can feel Logan staring at me as I clean the cut on the bottom of my foot and stick a bandage over it. My arm is still bleeding, but it's not too bad anymore so I wipe off the excess blood with a wad of toilet paper.

"That probably needs stitches," he says. I can see

that he's leaned up against the counter, his feet crossed at the ankles. But I don't dare look up. Looking him in the eyes is like feeding the delusion.

Ignoring him, I slap a band-aid over the cut. When that's done I just sit there for a minute with my eyes fixated on the spring behind the door. I'm trying to decide what to do, what to say. I squeeze my eyes shut and count to ten.

"Still here," he says when I open them. I sigh.

"Why?"

"Why what?"

"Why are you here?" I ask, finally looking up. "And what exactly are you?"

"Well, I'm here because for some weird reason you can see me when no one else can."

I sit back, still clutching the plastic first aid box to my chest.

"Why can I see you?"

He cocks his head, "How am I supposed to know?" He rubs his hand down his face in frustration, then glares at me. "Do you see dead people often?"

I make a face. "No. you're the first."

He throws his hands up. "Great. Just freaking great. The one person who can see me, and she has no clue what's going on." His eyes fall back to mine, "I was really hoping you'd have some answers."

"Well, I don't. So maybe you should just…you know. Go."

"Go where exactly?"

I stand up. "I don't know! Go into the light or something. Shit, what do I look like? A ghost expert?"

"You look like the only person who can see and hear me."

I let out a deep breath and squeeze the bridge of my nose with my thumb and forefinger. "This isn't happening. This is just some bad dream."

"Yeah, that's what I told myself too. For days I stood in my living room screaming at my parents while they sobbed over my picture. I thought I was losing my mind. Then I followed them to the funeral. And I saw you."

I flick my hands and he moves so I can toss the kit back under the sink. I turn and walk to my room with him following me.

"This is exactly why I don't go to funerals," I huff and flop onto my chair.

"*This* is why you don't go to funerals?" he asks, one eyebrow arched.

I shrug. "Fine, not *this* exactly. But nothing good ever comes from funerals. People are always like, *you should go, get some closure.* But that's all a load of crap. All it is, is another way to traumatize yourself. Just more bad memories to heap onto the pile."

He sits on the edge of my bed, Brimstone stands, arches her back in a stretch, then looks right at him, hisses and runs out of the room.

"Looks like you aren't the only one who can see me."

"That bi-polar cat is not proof that you aren't just a figment of my over caffeinated, over Poe'd imagination."

"This is getting old. How can I prove I'm really here?"

My head is beginning to ache. "I don't know. Being haunted is new to me, can you give me a minute to come to grips, *please?*"

He sits back on his hands. "Fine. One minute. Clock starts now."

I throw a pillow at him and it passes right through. "Well, I suppose I should have expected that," I mumble. He rolls his eyes.

I squint. "What are you in such a hurry for, anyway? You kind of have, I don't know, forever, right?"

Then something dawns on me. "Oh my God. You aren't going to haunt me forever, right? I mean, this isn't going to be my life now. Being followed around by an arrogant pain in the ass ghost?"

"Keep up the flattery and I just might."

I lean my head back and close my eyes. "I hate my life."

"You know, that's a pretty bitchy thing to say in front of a guy who no longer has one."

My head snaps up and I stare at him. I hadn't really thought of it that way. From his perspective, he must be miserable, in a special kind of hell.

"Sorry."

He shrugs it off, but I can still see traces of pain etched in the curve of his jaw.

His white and blue plaid shirt is open and exposing the grey t-shirt beneath. He's wearing a pair of khaki shorts and sneakers.

"Are you cold?" I ask without really thinking. Autumn air has come early and with the rain, it's probably below sixty degrees outside.

He looks down at his outfit. "Nope. I don't really feel temperature at all."

I tilt my head, "Why are you wearing clothes?"

His expression is surprised, then melts into a sly smile. "Why? Were you hoping for a naked haunting?"

I decide to take a page from Carlos's playbook. "Oh, honey, you don't have the figure for nudity."

He grins widely. "Oh, I really do."

I look him over and realize that he's right. He's not the skinny little boy who used to make mud castles in my back yard anymore. Even under his shirts, I can see the tell tale ribbons of muscle in his chest, shoulders, and arms, taught but defined. His jaw has squared in the last few years, filling out into a very masculine face. I look away when I see him staring at me as I appraise him. I try really hard not to look impressed.

"Well, I see your massive ego is still intact."

He leans to the side, sprawling out across my bed.

I glare, "No offense, but would you not do that on my bed?"

"What? Be sexy."

"No, be dead."

His face falls and he stands up. I immediately feel

bad, but this whole thing has me so weirded out that I have no idea what to say next.

"Oh, go ahead. I can practically see the hamster wheel in your brain smoking. Ask me whatever."

"Do you eat?"

"No. Not hungry either. Which is good, since I can't actually touch anything."

"What are you standing on? If you can't touch anything, what keeps your feet on the floor?"

He looks down at his sneakers and puckers his lips. "Good question. I don't know."

He squints and slips halfway down into my floor, only his upper half still visible. "Huh," he says, then floats up so he's hovering a few feet above the floor.

I wave my hands in front of my face. "No, no. Stop that. That's too creepy to process."

He shrugs and once again his feet are firmly on the ground.

"How do you get around? Do you just walk?"

"I can ride on things, in cars. I rode around with Kaylee for a few hours at first, in her Camero."

Probably screaming at her too, hoping that she, that anyone, could hear him. Oh, lucky me.

"But," he continues, "After I saw you leave the wake, I waited around to see everyone pay their respects."

"That must have been strange."

Uncomfortable, awful. Or, maybe in his case, a huge ego trip. The face he gives me tells me my first thoughts are closer to accurate.

"People wanted to say goodbye. I figured I should give them the chance."

I nod. "I'm sorry."

He frowns, "Why?"

"I dunno. For calling you a douche wrench at your own funeral." For not caring that you died. I want to say the words, but I can't get them out.

"Douche hammer. You called me a douche hammer."

I shrug. "I knew it was some kind of tool."

"Well, we weren't exactly close."

"And face it, you are a tool."

I take a deep breath. The summer before middle school my parents took me on vacation to visit my uncle in Paris for the summer. It was amazing, but when I got back, Logan had a new group of friends. And I was the odd girl out. Then, a few months into school, my father go into a car accident and died. Mom pulled me out to home school for the rest of that year. I just couldn't face anyone for a while. By the time 8th grade began, Logan and I were like total strangers. He was Mr. Popular. And I was nobody.

"I guess the million dollar question then Is - What *exactly* do you want from me?"

He squats near my feet, looking up at me. "When you saw me at the funeral, I was terrified. Because that meant that I was really dead, not just having some prolonged nightmare. But then I was relieved too because, I guess, I hoped that you could help me."

"Help you what?"

He scratches his chin. "I dunno. Help me figure all this out. Help me just...not be so alone."

I lean forward. "Why should I? Like you said, we aren't friends."

He rocks back on his heels. "We used to be."

"That was a long time ago."

"Well, how about this. You're going to have to pee some time. And when you do, I'll be there."

I make a face. "Fine. Where do we start?"

"Where all strange and possibly evil things begin. Wikipedia."

Three

I TAKE A LONG GULP OF MY ENERGY DRINK. My room is dark except for the blue glow provided by my computer screen. Sitting back in my desk chair, I stretch and roll my head to the sides and crack my neck.

"Anything?" Logan asks behind me.

I spin in my chair. "If I'd found something I would have said *Hey. I found something.*"

"You know, you're really cranky for being the only person in the room who has a body." I turn back to the screen and flip him off over my shoulder, "Keep flapping your lips and you'll spend the rest of your afterlife haunting hipsters at Starbucks."

"Oh, sure. Threaten the dead guy."

I sigh and lower my head onto the keyboard. It's after 4 a.m. and even after sleeping all day, I'm exhausted.

"Isn't there someone else you can haunt for a few hours."

He stands beside me, leaning over the desk. "Everyone is sleeping. Besides, it's just depressing."

I roll my face to the side to look at him. "Being dead?"

He frowns, not looking at me. "Watching everyone else be alive."

I sit up, slapping my hands down on either side of the keyboard.

"Okay, I have a plan."

I spin in my chair and accidently graze him. Well, graze is the wrong word. I move through him. A chill runs up my skin and goosebumps erupt across my arms like tiny volcanoes.

I pull back, rubbing my arms. "Well, that was disturbing."

He shakes his head. "The plan?"

"Oh. Right. I think we should try going to the cemetery."

He leans back, looking worried. "Why? You want me to try to climb back into my body?"

I think about that for a second. "No. I don't think that's a good idea. I mean, the goal isn't to make you a zombie, right? Just to find your light or whatever."

"My light?"

"Yeah, you know." He stares at me like I'm an idiot. "When people die they see a light. *Go into the light* and all that."

"I don't remember a light."

I fold my hands on my lap. "What do you remember?"

"About dying? Nothing. I remember opening my

eyes and the police were dragging my body out of the water. I remember screaming and no one hearing me. Then I thought about my mom and suddenly I was in my house, standing beside her. She was on the floor, crying."

That's interesting. "How did you get into my room?"

He rubs his forehead. "I was thinking of you, how you saw me at the funeral. Then, I was just here."

Convenient.

"Okay. I think we should go to the cemetery because, well, maybe there are other ghosts there who can help you. You can't be the only person who ever took a wrong turn heading for the afterlife."

He looks up, considering it. "And you think you could see them?"

"No, but maybe you can."

He nods, "That makes sense."

I stand up and head for my closet. "It's a place to start, at least."

Grabbing a pair of pants and a t-shirt off the hangars I turn to see him staring at me.

"Let's do it." He says, clapping his hands together.

I pucker my lips. "Yeah, well, I have to get dressed first so you should, you know, turn around. Or go outside. Or something."

He slaps his hand over his eyes. I put a balled up fist on my hip. "Nice try Casper."

With a frustrated sigh he vanishes and I hear him calling from my kitchen. "Prude."

"Perv," I call back, slipping into my jeans.

Once I'm fully dressed, I grab my car keys and head out. It's a good thing Mom is working a double shift. She'd kill me if she knew I was heading out to the cemetery in the middle of the night. And if I tried to explain why, she'd have me committed.

"What are you thinking about?" Logan asks as we drive slowly up to the front gate of Stone Hill Cemetery.

I lean over the dash, looking at the towering wrought iron gate and the thick chains binding it closed. "You really want to talk about my feelings, Logan?"

He slides through the door without opening it and stands in front of my head lights. "Pathetic as it is, talking to you has kind of been the highlight of my week. So, yeah."

I kill the lights and slam the door of my old yellow VW Beetle closed. "Aw, that's kinda sweet. You know, in a not really sort of way."

He rolls his eyes. In three long strides he steps toward the black iron bars and runs right into them. Stepping back, he looks stunned. In my mind something clicks into place.

"Ghosts can't pass through iron," I say, feeling smug. He turns and stares at me. I shrug. "I saw it on TV."

He reaches for the bar and wraps his hand around it. As soon as he does his hand begins to smoke like its burning. He yelps, pulls his hand back and rubs it.

"I guess I can feel some things."

I nod and walk up beside him. "Yeah, iron is like

ghost kryptonite. Hey, we should dig up your body, then pour salt on it and light it on fire."

He stares at me, his nose crinkled up. "Why?"

"To release your spirit."

"I'm pretty released, thanks."

"Still."

"We are not desecrating my corpse based on something you saw on TV."

I frown. "You have no sense of whimsy, you know that?"

He rolls his eyes and points to a stone wall. "There, we can get in over there. You'll have to climb it."

Of course I will. I run back to the car and grab a flashlight off the floorboard, tucking it into my back pocket. As I watch, he steps through the wall.

"All clear," he whispers.

"You don't have to whisper, no one can hear you."

"Oh, right. I forgot."

I shake my head. This has got to be the absolute top of the list of the stupidest things I've ever done. As a matter of fact, this might actually *be* the list. Clinging carefully to each stone, I climb up. Luckily it's not very high, but my arms still feel like lead weights when I jump over the other side and land gingerly on my feet.

"Like a ninja," I whisper as Logan smiles. It's a warm, sincere smile, something I haven't seen him wear in a long time—which is a shame because it looks really good on him.

"Where to now?" I ask, dusting off my hands on

my jeans.

He shrugs and starts walking. Not sure what else to do, I follow him. We wander past the old, battered headstones toward the newer part of the cemetery which is in the very back. The paths are all old cobblestone, giant obelisks and weeping angels looking down on us as we walk. We pass by a small crypt and I shine the flashlight on the entrance. Over the gate, carved in stone is the phrase, *Verum non est in morte.*

"What does it say?" Logan asks from behind me.

I know the translation, not because I can read Latin, but because I'd asked my mother the same question as we were leaving my father's funeral.

"It says, *In death there is truth.*"

Lowering my light, I shine it around, over the headstones. "Do you see anything?"

He shakes his head. "No. Nothing."

I sigh, defeated. We walk on until we see a big yellow back hoe parked next to a fresh grave. Logan freezes but I walk closer, shining the light on the name etched into the stone.

Logan Wayne Cooper.

I turn, shining the light on Logan. "Wayne, really?"

He looks away, "My dad likes old westerns."

"Huh." I step around the grave, careful not to disturb the freshly mounded dirt or the stacks of fresh flowers. "I hear they take these flowers and give them to the old people at the nursing home," I say, desperate to break the silence. He doesn't answer. When I glance up his back is to me. The moonlight is hitting him at an odd angle, making him almost glow. It's so beautiful that for a moment I'm transfixed by it. He looks over his shoulder at me and all I can think is how beautiful he is. Like an angel.

Then he opens his mouth.

"What are you staring at?"

I roll my eyes. "Just wondering if you're going to do something or just stand there sparkling like an idiot."

"What do you want me to do?" he asks, throwing his hands in the air.

I inhale slowly. "You said you thought of me, and then you were just there, in my room, right?"

"Yeah." He turns, walking toward me.

I shift from one foot to the other. "Well, maybe you should think of…I dunno…heaven. Or whatever."

"Heaven?" He snorts.

"Don't get an attitude with me, there buddy. I'm standing in a cemetery at five in the morning next to a fresh grave talking to a dead guy. My tolerance has its limits."

"Fine." He grumbles. He closes his eyes takes a deep breath and…

Nothing.

He opens one eye. Then his face falls. "This was a stupid idea."

"Your face is stupid."

He stomps away, tugging on his hair. Then he spins back, pointing at me. "You know, you are such a joy to be around. I can't imagine why you don't have any friends."

That hurts. "I have friends," I whisper.

"Oh, I forgot. Gay Carlos tolerates you. That doesn't make you his friend. It makes you his hag."

The pain from his words is so quick and so sharp it feels like he slapped me in the face. I recover quickly, the pain feeding my already growing anger.

"Listen up you pompous ass waffle. Number one, don't you ever talk about Carlos that way again. He's worth ten of you. And two, you can take your afterlife drama and shove it. Don't come to my house, don't ever bother me again. I mean it. You are on your own." Turning my back on him I march out of the cemetery, scale the wall, and drive home, fighting back tears of rage the whole way.

By the time I'm settling into bed the sun is rising, casting a red-orange glow into my room. I grab the curtains and pull them closed, falling into bed still in my clothes. A knock at my door wakes me.

"Hey Zoe Bowie. You up yet?"

I glance at the alarm. 8:46 Am. Son of a—

"Come on in Carlos."

He pokes his head around the door, his eyes covered by his hand. "You decent?"

I shrug, "As decent as I ever am."

He laughs and walks in. He's holding a drink carrier with two tall Starbucks cups and has a bag of croissants tucked under his arm.

"I brought fuel." He hands me the cup. I can tell from the smell its Earl Grey tea with honey and cream.

"Bless you, kind sir." I murmur and take a sip. It's hot enough to burn the tip of my tongue a little—just how I like it.

"Oh honey, what did you get up to last night?"

I arch an eyebrow. "Why do you ask?"

He waves his hand over me, "Well, you look like you've been held in a basement for three days and you have bags under your eyes the size of cantaloupes."

"Yeah, I didn't sleep much." I play with the lid on my drink, unsure what to say. No way in hell am I going to admit that I've been seeing Logan. As much as I love Carlos, it just feels too crazy to admit out loud. Still, I kind of need to talk to someone about it.

"I've been thinking about Logan."

He looks surprised. Pulling off his grey canvas jacket he scoots down beside me.

"I thought you didn't care about all that."

I shrug.

"I don't. It's just… I dunno. Maybe it's bringing up old feelings…of when dad died."

Carlos lays a hand on my knee sympathetically. He came into my life just a few months after Dad's funeral. He moved in down the block and my mom made me take over a welcome to the neighborhood pie. I remember how scared he was, how freaked out about being in a new town, at a new school. But Carlos is braver than me. He stepped in on day one and made himself known. He never hid who he was or what he wanted. I wish I had that kind of courage.

I take another drink. My head is writhing with questions, questions I know Carlos can't answer.

His face lights up, "I know what you need."

Yeah, a nice long vacation somewhere with padded rooms and happy pills.

"That makes one of us," I mumble.

"How about we take a drive up Skyline, have a picnic, then go down to the Tea Room?"

I feel the sides of my mouth turn up slowly. "That actually sounds really nice."

He grins, looking quite pleased with himself. "I know." Then he lowers his gaze at me, pointing up and down. "But first you shower and change. I'm not taking you anywhere looking like that."

I agree and he goes off to the kitchen to scavenge some food for our picnic. Knowing what's in my cabinets, we might be dining on mustard and old soda crackers.

Forty five minutes later I'm clean and dressed in my soft tan cargo pants and a black tank top and Carlos has plaited my hair into a long French braid.

The drive up Skyline is a soothing one, even with Carlos's indie rock blasting through the speakers of his dad's Four Runner. The sky is clear and blue—the shade of blue you can't find anywhere else on earth—and the sun is bright and warm on my arm as it dangles out the window. We drive until we hit the very top of the mountain, a place called the Garden of the Gods. It's a large field filled with trees as big around as a truck. I spread out a plaid blanket while he retrieves the picnic basket and a bottle of sparkling wine from his trunk.

"Fancy," I say realizing that this day's events weren't as spur of the moment as he'd led me to believe.

"It's a celebration. To the first day of the rest of our lives."

He twists off the top and bubbles ooze out, sliding down the side of the bottle, which he hands me. "Sorry, I forgot to pack glasses."

I shrug and take a small sip. It's smooth and tastes vaguely like apples. "Not bad."

He winks and takes the bottle from me.

"You sure you should be drinking?" I ask, knowing that the drive down will be a windy one.

"I'll just have a touch. Besides, I'm used to it." He takes a small sip and hands it back to me before opening the basket. His family is one of those European types who have wine with every meal, even the kids, so his tolerance is pretty high.

As it turns out, he was able to make quite a little feast with leftovers and creativity. By the time the food was gone we'd drank about a third of the bottle and were lying back, relaxing in the sun.

"Do you think people can haunt you?" I ask quietly.

Carlos rolls onto his side, propping his head on his elbow so he's practically pressed against me. With anyone else the closeness would feel intimate, but with Carlos it just feels comforting.

"Yeah, I do."

"Really?"

"Sure. I think sometimes we hold onto people so tightly, we can feel them around us all the time."

I sigh. That's not quite what I meant.

"What about, like ghosts?"

"Ghosts?" his tone is concerned.

Ah, crap.

"Yeah, I mean, do you think that sometimes when people die, they can just, sort of…I dunno. Still be here?"

He rolls onto his back, clasping his hands behind his head.

"If the Sci-fi channel has taught us anything, it's that ghosts are everywhere." He chuckles. "All those poor souls and their unfinished business."

I look over at him. "Unfinished business?"

"Yeah, that's what keeps them here, at least according those guys on the ghost hunting show. They have stuff they still need to do or something."

"I didn't know you watched that crap," I joke lightly, letting his words roll around in my head.

"Don't judge me." He chuckles. "Why do you ask anyway? You feeling haunted?"

I decide to be as honest as I can. "I feel like, sometimes, I can still hear him. Logan I mean. Or I see him out the corner of my eye."

"I was that way when my little brother died. For the first little while, it was like I could feel him in the house. Every once in a while, I was sure I'd seen him, but it was always just my mind playing tricks."

I remember the feeling. That had happened when my dad died too. Rolling over I nuzzle my head into his chest and let him rub my back until I fall asleep.

I'm dreaming of the cemetery, of Logan's face as I screamed at him. Behind him, one of the stone angels was walking forward, sword in hand. She stopped behind him and lifted the sword over his head like she was going to cut him in half.

The crash of thunder wakes me an instant before the now dark sky opens up and begins to pour. I grab the basket as Carlos grabs the blanket and we race for the car, laughing. As soon as I'm in and buckled I look out the window and see Logan standing on the side of the road, staring at me. The smile falls off my face.

By the time we make it to the Tea Room I'm mostly dry. We pull into the narrow lot and park. Carlos reaches into the back seat and pulls out his guitar.

"Open mic?" I ask hopefully.

He smiles widely.

Inside, beyond the initial sitting room that's all decked out in long red velvet couches and high backed Victorian chairs, the space opens into an area stuffed with small round bistro tables. The walls are covered in gold and bronze gilded mirrors and shelves that are overflowing with ornate vases, candle sticks, and other antiques. I head straight for the table in the back corner, the dimmest corner of the room. On the table, a single candle flickers in a frosted glass mason jar. Out of nowhere Lana ,the owner and resident tea expert, appears. Lana is about four and a half feet tall, with her long raven hair rolled along her hairline in a 1950's style wave. Her skin is creased with age, her eyes narrow and warm brown. She throws her arms around me—something she does to all the regulars—and the smell of her thick lavender perfume sticks to me even after she moves on to embrace Carlos.

"I'm so glad to see you!" she says warmly, just a hint of a Korean accent in her voice. "Sit, sit."

We slide into our chairs and she gently takes the guitar out of Carlos's hand.

"I'll put this by the stage for you."

Taking her free hand to her chin she squints at me.

"You'll try the mango ginger tonight, I think. And you, raspberry and honey?"

We both nod and smile. The first time we came I made the mistake of asking for a menu and she just rambled off about fifty teas before telling me what I would have. Since then we never actually get to order for ourselves, she just sort of chooses for us. I don't really mind. Three years of coming here and she has yet to serve me something I don't like.

Carlos watches her carefully lean his guitar next

to the old jukebox near the stage. The stage is little more than a four foot square of tile with a microphone plugged into an old amp and a faded red stool on it. But this is Carlos's favorite place to play. It's quiet and intimate and the acoustics are somehow perfect.

Turning back quickly, he jerks his head over his shoulder. "He's here."

My head snaps to attention. For one idiotic second I think he means Logan. I glance around and don't see him. "Who?" I ask, confused.

"Behind me to the left. No, my left."

I glance over. The hot guy from Bloomingdales is here with two friends.

"Did you…?"

He bristles. "I may have mentioned that I come here to play sometimes. But I certainly didn't *invite* him."

"Why not?"

He tugs the front of his grey vest. "If I'd known he was coming, I would have—"

"Chickened out?"

He raises a shoulder, touching it to his chin in a sassy gesture, "Worn my good blue shirt."

"Are you still going to sing?" I ask, sitting forward with my elbows on the table.

He rakes a hand through his dark hair. "Of course I am. Maybe. After my tea."

No sooner does he say the words than Lana comes tottering over with a silver tray. She carefully sets two empty cups on the table in front of us, places a copper tea ball in each one, then lays out the cream, sugar, spoons, and a small plate of fresh lavender scones.

"Let them steep five minutes," she orders before turning around and heading to another table to deliver a ticket.

We add the hot water from the small white kettle and wait, knowing full well not obeying her recommended steep time will earn us sharp looks from her later.

Stirring a spoon of sugar into his tea Carlos begins telling me about his audition for Rhett in this year's production. He wants me to run lines. I smile and agree, knowing that for the third year in a row he will end up as Ashley. Not masculine enough for Rhett is what they tell him. I think they're just assholes.

"So I was thinking of growing out a beard," he says, finally taking a sip. "Not a weird hillbilly beard, but one of those, *oh I just didn't have time to shave this week* beards."

I'm only half listening. Part of my brain is still thinking about what he said earlier, about unfinished business. Could that really be what's holding Logan here? And if so, what does he need to do to resolve it? I must be staring off into space because the next thing I know, Carlos is snapping his fingers in my face.

"Hello, earth to Zoe?"

"What? Sorry."

"I asked if you had a back to school entrance strategy."

I take a long sip of my tea only to pucker when I

realize I've forgotten to put any sugar in it. "You make it sound like we're planning a military invasion."

He sits back, resting his chin in one hand. "Oh, Zoe. You are so sweet. That's exactly what it is. An invasion of a hostile country. You can try for diplomacy, or you can just go in with guns blazing." He pauses, giving me a pointed look. "You realize that you could have your pick of any guy in school, right?"

I raise one eyebrow. "Did someone spike your tea?"

"I'm serious. Honey, listen. You have this sort of shell of bitchiness that you hide behind. If you would just open up and let the rest of the world see you the way that I do…"

He trails off. I make a face and stick out my tongue.

"Okay, maybe not exactly how I see you, but you get my drift. I mean, you're smart, funny, pretty. If it weren't for your acidic mouth you could be the most popular girl in school."

I roll my eyes.

"He's right." Logan chimes in and I nearly drop my teacup in my lap, choking on the hot liquid.

"You alright there Zoe?" Carlos asks.

I cough into my napkin. He stands to pat my back but I wave him off.

"I'm fine. Wrong pipe. Sorry."

"You sure you're ok? I could Heimlich you if you want."

He sits back down, his eyes are glinting

mischievously.

"Thanks but I'll pass." I nod to the table up front. "Maybe Bloomie Hottie will choke and you can Heimlich him."

Carlos sighs wistfully. "We can only hope."

Logan takes a seat in the empty chair beside me, passing through the table to get to it. I try not to look at him.

"Ignoring me now?" he says lightly.

I frown but don't answer.

"Blink once if you can hear me," he says with a chuckle.

I scratch the side of my head with my middle finger. He laughs harder.

This is getting old fast.

I nod to the stage, "Alright, enough stalling. Go sing for me."

With a wide grin Carlos gets up, leaning over the table to press a quick kiss on my forehead before heading for the stage. He sits down and settles himself in. As soon as he plucks the first chord I'm transfixed. The entire room falls into silence, the only sound is the melody he plays. Closing his eyes he sings one of my favorite songs, a cover of *All We Are We Are* by Matt Nathanson.

I take a deep breath and let the sound of his voice wash over me.

"He's really good," Logan says.

I don't even look at him.

"Ok, you are still pissed. I get it. And…I'm sorry. I

shouldn't have said those things. I didn't mean any of it."

I take my last sip of tea and slide my cup back.

"Come on, Zoe. Please don't shut me out. I was upset. I didn't mean it."

I shift in my seat, letting my hair fall forward into my face as I whisper.

"Yes, you did."

"No, I really didn't. Carlos is a good guy, and he's lucky to have a friend like you."

I shake my head slowly, not ready to forgive him just yet.

"Carlos is right, you know. You do have this armor around yourself. You should let people in more."

I turn and glare at him. "Why? All people ever do is let me down or abandon me. Why should I let anyone in? It's not worth it."

"You let Carlos in."

"I let you in too. Look how well that worked out."

He frowns and lowers his chin. It looks like he wants to say something, but can't quite figure out the words.

"Do you really want to live that way?" he asks finally.

I shrug and turn back to Carlos. He finishes the last chords and the room erupts into applause.

He stands up and takes a quick bow. Before he can step off the stage Bloomie Hottie stands and stops him, they chat and Carlos busts out his million dollar smile. That poor cashier is toast.

I sigh. "I'm sorry too, Logan. I'm sure being dead is very stressful. Look, I think I might know why you're still stuck here. Meet me at my house in an hour and we will talk then."

"Where should I go in the mean time?" his voice is tight, on the cusp of whiny. "Not that I'm having tons of fun hanging here with you."

I glare at him for a second.

"I can make a suggestion, but you'll need a handbasket."

Four

B Y THE TIME CARLOS DROPS ME OFF its full dark, not a star in the sky thanks to the still dense clouds. My head is buzzing with his excitement over his upcoming date with Bloomie Hottie—aka Scott. Mom's car is in the driveway, but the house is dark except for the small light over the kitchen sink. When I get in, there's a carton of Orange Chicken and rice and a post-it note with, *Have a good night* scrawled across it. Mom's idea of an apology since she hates Chinese food. I grab a fork and the food and head for my room. Flicking on the light with my elbow I expect to see Logan sitting there, but he isn't. I glance at my alarm clock. I'm actually a little late. It's been almost an hour and a half since I saw him at the tea room.

Maybe he's finally gone.

I stab at my food as an uncomfortable knot forms in my stomach.

"That smells really good," his voice says behind me. I spin in my chair and Logan is standing in my doorway, leaning against the wall.

"Nice of you to show up." I mutter around a bite of chicken. Then I frown, realizing what he said. "Wait, you can still smell things?"

He makes a show of inhaling deeply through his nose. "Orange chicken, right?"

I nod.

"Then, yeah. I guess so."

I raise one eyebrow. "That's so weird. I mean, you can hear and see and smell, so why can't you feel anything, like, touch. All your other senses seem to be functioning."

He rolls his eyes and steps into the room, "I don't know. I'm pretty new at this whole being dead thing, remember."

I point the fork at him. "Right. About that..."

Spinning in my chair as I hit my mouse and my laptop flickers to life. I set the canister of food aside and type. I don't feel Logan slide up beside me, but he leans over me, propping himself up with one arm on my desk.

"What are you searching?"

"Carlos thinks you might have unfinished business, something keeping you here."

I don't look up as the search results roll in. I click on a video link and it's one of those paranormal investigators from TV doing an interview.

"Most of the spirits we encounter are trapped here in a perpetual loop, searching for some kind of closure that will allow them to move on. Sometimes, we can assist with that search—help them find peace..."

"Hey," I nudge Logan like an idiot, my shoulder passing right through his. "Maybe you should go haunt this dude. He seems to know what he's doing."

Logan shushes me while I make a face at him.

The host continues, *"Most of the time, these spirits don't even know they're dead. It's sad really, but it happens, particularly in cases of sudden or violent deaths."*

The video fades out and Logan steps back.

"Zoe, how did I die?"

I spin around to face him, unable to keep the shock out of my voice. "You really don't remember?"

His face is twisted, like he's trying to reach something and can't quite grasp it. Finally, he shakes his head.

"Oh, maybe you should sit down." I say, a mixture of guilt and sympathy coiling inside me.

He cocks his head at me in an *oh please* gesture.

I hold up my hands. "Fine."

I sit back and stretch out my legs, kicking off my ballet flats.

"The word around town is that it was an accident. You were over on the Tower Bridge and fell into the river and drowned."

"I fell off the bridge?"

I nod.

He shakes his head and turns his back to me.

"That doesn't make any sense. I never go on that bridge."

I shrug. "Well, you did."

"No, you don't understand. I'm afraid of heights. Remember the year your dad put in that tree house?"

I jerk, suprised by the memory. We were seven and my dad spent all summer building me a tree house in the back yard. No matter how I begged, Logan would never go inside. Taking a deep breath I push the swelling tide of emotions away. It's a trick I've gotten very good at over the years. If you can bury the sadness deep enough, and pile enough distraction on top of it, you don't have to feel it—don't have to deal with it.

My mouth twitches. "Then what happened?"

He blows out a frustrated breath. "I don't remember."

"Ok, what is the last thing you do remember?"

He sits on the edge of my bed, "I remember… going to the pool party at Bruno's house."

Kyle Bruno is one of Logan's friends, one of the Lacrosse jocks. I heard about the party, even got an invite online-probably a mistake-but I didn't go. Parade around in a swim suit for the meat heads to ogle? No thank you.

"That was almost a month ago." I point out grimly. "Are you sure you wouldn't have gone out on that bridge for any reason?"

He levels a serious look at me, lowering his chin, "Nothing short of being shot at would have gotten me onto that bridge. And maybe not even that."

"So, do you think maybe this is your unfinished business? Finding out what happened to you?"

He rubs his hand down his face. "Yeah. Maybe. I

don't know. It's as good a theory as any."

I spin back around to the computer and pull up his iFriend page. "What's your password?"

He pauses, making me glare at him over my shoulder.

"Do you want my help or not? If we are going to figure out what happened to you, we should start by looking at your posts and messages from around that time."

He sighs. "It's *r o x s t a r r # 1*."

I roll my eyes. "Of course it is."

"You know, you're pretty judgmental for a chick with a stuffed unicorn on her bed."

"Bite me, ghost boy."

"If I could, I just might."

"Problem. Your account has been deleted," I say, exiting and trying to log in again, just to be sure. "I pulled up an archived page, but it's just the wall. Aww, look. People wrote such nice things about you. They must not have known you very well."

He shrugs, "It's martyr syndrome. Like when someone dies, all you can remember about them is the good stuff. So in death, you get to be perfect."

"Is that a real thing?" I ask lightly, keeping a tight lid on those pesky inner emotions trying to crawl their way out.

"Yeah. Like I had this uncle who died. He was an a-class asshole while he was alive. Everyone hated him. I think they felt so guilty when he died, they all said nice things about him at his funeral to make themselves feel better."

I turn back to Logan who is poking at my unicorn experimentally, his hand moving right through it each time.

"Going through your account is out. Do you think you have any emails or texts we can go through?"

"I never used my email. And I have no idea what happened to my phone. They only found my wallet."

I frown, wondering how he knows that. Seeing the question written all over my face he elaborates.

"I remember seeing them—when they pulled my body out of the water—they took it out of my pocket and put it in one of those evidence bags. But there was no phone."

My mouth forms a silent O.

"So if we can't access your texts or messages, how are we supposed to reconstruct your last few weeks, much less your…"

"You can say it. Death."

"I was actually going to say murder."

Now it's his turn to wear the confused face. I shrug.

"Look, if you didn't go into that water of your own volition, and if you didn't accidentally fall in—"

I don't say anything else. His skin has paled—though I'm not sure how that's possible—and he looks visibly shaken. Leaning forward with his elbows on his knees, he stares at my beige carpet. He's shaking his head softly.

"Who would want me dead?" he whispers.

I raise my hand.

He glances up and laughs.

"Why am I not surprised by that?"

Lowering my arm I pick at my fingernails.

"Well, you do irritate me."

"Yeah, but did I annoy you when I was alive?"

I think about that for a second. "No, I suppose not. It's hard to annoy someone who doesn't even orbit the same planet as you. Or maybe you're just annoying dead?"

He smirks, "Well I never had any complaints while I was alive so, maybe. Then again, maybe you just bring out the best in me."

I pucker. That's entirely possible. Lord knows Carlos has called me abrasive more than once.

Changing the subject I stab a piece of chicken and hold it out to Logan.

"Ok, experiment time."

He looks around the fork at me like I've lost my mind.

"Lick it." I say.

"You lick it."

I sigh, "Seriously. If we are going to work with the whole ghost thing, I'd like to know the rules. I want to see if you can taste it."

"Why? Are you planning on having me lick things often?"

I thrust the fork forward, "Just do it."

Reluctantly he leans forward and sticks out his tongue, making a licking sound like a dog.

"Anything?" I ask hopefully.

"Maybe just a little? But I might just be smelling it through my mouth."

"Huh."

I stare at the fork for a second, debating whether to eat it or put it back in the box. I mean, he didn't get his germs on it or anything, did he? Do ghosts even have germs? Ghost cooties?

He's watching me with an amused expression. I shrug and take the bite, stuffing the empty fork back in the carton. He grins, obviously pleased.

"So, really, who wanted you dead?" I ask. "I mean, besides me. Who did you tick off recently?"

He flops down on my bed, folding his hands across his stomach and staring at the ceiling.

"I have no idea. But I think I have an idea how we can find out."

I lean to the side, propping my chin up with my fist. "Enlighten me."

"You need to talk to my friends," he says as if it's the most obvious, simple thing in the world.

"You mean that bunch of people that I've never spoken to in my life? Those friends."

He rolls his head to the side, looking at me. "Yeah. Why not?"

I'm totally caught off guard by the suggestion. It's

like asking a fish to talk to a bird.

"Sure, I'll just walk up to Kaylee's door and say, *Hey I know this is a little weird, but your boyfriend is kind of haunting me and he wants to know what you guys did right before he died, because he thinks someone killed him.* She would have me arrested. Or committed. Or both."

"She'd just pepper spray you."

"Also something I'd like to avoid."

He looks away again. "No. School starts in a few days. We need to figure out a way to get you into the inner circle, make you part of the group."

I feel my eyes go buggy. "Oh hell no. Hell. No."

"You already said you'd help."

I sigh, leaning back. "I didn't say I'd let you throw me to the lions."

"They aren't that bad."

I stare at him. He's obviously in some kind of death induced denial. One bad word from Kaylee alone could blackball me from any event or club for the rest of the year. Granted, student council isn't glamorous, but I need it on my college applications. Plus there was always the very real possibility she might scratch my eyes out. I've seen her do worse.

"We will start with Bruno."

I sigh. I'm not winning this argument, I can just tell. This is my life now, being bullied and stalked by a dead guy. Lucky me.

"Why him?"

"He asked me for your number at the end of last

year. I think he's got a little thing for you."

My mouth hangs open. I couldn't have been more surprised if he started belching puppies.

"He never called me."

Logan waves me off with a flick of his hand. "He's shy. Probably couldn't get up the nerve."

Bruno is a good looking guy, I have to admit. He's one of those muscular dudes with a dark tan and dimples. Somehow boyishly cute and brutally handsome in the same breath, and of all Logan's friends, he is also the only one who has ever looked me right in the eye instead of looking right through me. It was in Pre-calculus last year. He asked me for some notes he missed. He smiled when he handed them back to me. And I never thought anything of it. Until now, that is. Now it feels like a flashing neon sign I'd somehow overlooked.

"What are you thinking?" Logan asks, shaking me from the not so unpleasant memory. I shake my head. No way. Bruno was probably just looking for a summer tutor.

"I'm thinking there is no way that your pack of lemmings will accept me as one of them. Not in a million years."

"Don't sell yourself short. You're smart, funny in a sour way, and even kinda pretty. You just need…"

I'm trying to read the expression on his face.

"A flea bath?" I finish, judging by the wrinkled up nose and narrowed eyes he's giving me, I assume those are his next words.

"I was going to say an image adjustment."

His words sting more than I let him see. "Oh really?"

"Yep. Some new clothes, a little sunshine or makeup or something so you don't look so pale. A hair cut. You know, a makeover. Don't girls love makeovers?"

I leap out on my chair and squeal, kneeling beside the bed. "Yeah, in cheesy 80's movies. And are you going to be my fairy godmother and make me a dress for the ball, too?"

"Wrong movie."

I rock back on my heels and put my hands on my hips. "Wait, is this the movie where I go to prom only to have a bucket of pigs blood poured on me?"

He rolls to his side and props himself up on one elbow. "Wrong again. This is the movie where you ask your best friend to help you polish yourself up so you can earn yourself a place in the herd and figure out who killed me."

"So My Fair Lady, Ghost Hunters edition. How does it end?"

"With at least one of us dead."

I put a finger to my lips and shhh him. "Spoiler."

Five

I lay awake in my bed long after I've sent Logan on his merry way. Staring at the ceiling, wondering what left turn I've taken to land myself in this particular pot of crazy. When I finally fall into a restless sleep, I dream of Logan when he was alive. We were in the hall at school, crowds of people buzzing around us like wasps, glaring. But we just stand there, our eyes glued on one another across the room. A person in a black hoodie walks up behind him, raises a massive knife and starts slashing him in the back. I scream but no sound comes out. Logan doesn't flinch, even as the blood sprays the lockers behind him. Then the people around us stop, turn away from me, and watch in frozen silence as Logan crumples to the ground in a bloody heap. I scream again but I can't move. When the faces turn back to me, they are all covered in blood.

I jolt awake, nearly flinging myself out of bed. Three times last night the dream had been the same. And each time I woke as I was now, sweaty and flushed, my heart pounding like drums in my chest. I slam my hand down on the wailing alarm clock, but even once it's dead the sound vibrates inside my skull. I groan, squeezing my eyes shut and wondering if this is what a hangover feels like.

"Good morning sleepy head."

I let out a startled noise and trip backward, landing on my butt.

"For shit's sake, don't do that." I say finally as Logan stands over me chuckling.

He holds out his hand like he's going to help me up. I raise an eyebrow at the gesture.

"Really?"

He shrugs and drops his hand, walking away.

"Oh, right. I forgot."

I struggle to my feet and he drops into my sitting chair. "So, were you dreaming about me? You kept saying my name in your sleep."

"How long have you been here?" I accuse, narrowing my eyes.

He waves me off. "A while. I got bored. Nowhere else to go."

I turn my back to him, sliding open my closet. "Stalker."

"You know, you should be flattered. I mean I could be stalking anybody right now. Cool people."

I yawn and pull a pair of dark jeans and my soft grey Henley off of their hangers.

"Yes. Lucky me. And to think, you're passing up

the opportunity to literally be a fly on the wall at the playboy mansion right now just to hang out here and irritate me into an early grave."

A knock at my door makes me jump. Mom peeks her head in, looking around.

"Hey, what are you doing in here?" She widens the door a little, checking behind it. "I thought I heard you talking to someone."

I sigh, "No mom, just…practicing my lines. Carlos is making me try out for *Gone with the Wind* with him this year."

The lie comes out smoother than I expect. I think I can count the number of times I've lied to my mother on one hand, that is, if you don't count all the times she's asked me how I'm doing and I say, *Fine mom. Everything's great.* Because those lies would number in the thousands.

She gives me a wary half smile. It's hard to tell if she's not buying it, or if she's just exhausted. She's been working double and triple shifts at the hospital for months. I get why. Idle time is when the pain creeps back in. Happens to me too. Maybe that's why I agreed to help Logan. Maybe I just need a distraction.

Mom walks into my room and puts her arms around me in an awkward hug as I try to hug her back with one arm while still holding onto my clothes.

"You doing okay?" She asks, brushing the hair out of my face.

"Sure mom. I'm fine."

She nods and takes a step back. "Have you done

your back to school shopping yet?"

"I'm going to see if Carlos wants to go today."

Her eyes brighten and I turn away. She adores Carlos.

Hell, who doesn't?

"Well you two have fun. I'm going to put together a dessert for the staff barbeque tonight. Did you want to come with me?"

I frown where she can't see me. Truth is I'd rather be raked naked over hot coals than spend five minutes with her colleagues from the hospital. Between the gossipy nurses, rude orderlies, and Doctor Tucker, the resident surgeon who always leers at my mom right in front of his poor wife, a fork to the eyeball sounds more fun.

"I think Carlos wants to go to some poetry reading at the tea room tonight."

Another lie. Wow, I'm really on a roll today.

"Hey, your mom is really trying to spend time with you. You should go." Logan chimes in from the chair. I grit my teeth and ignore him.

"Oh, well, ok then. I suppose I'll see you tomorrow after my shift."

I nod, not turning back to her as she leaves, closing the door behind her.

"You know, if you die tomorrow and those were the last words you said to her, you would feel like shit. Trust me, I know."

"Ground rules. Number one, no watching me

sleep like a perv. And number two, no guilt trips about my relationship with my mom—or anyone else for that matter. Keep any and all urges to be my undead life coach to yourself. Clear?"

He nods. I turn on my heel and head for the bathroom. I need a shower and five minutes away from all of the people talking in my head, living and dead.

I dress in the bathroom, which I never do, because I don't want to risk my pervy little buddy catching a peek. I'm self conscious enough about my tall, overly skinny body without him making any comments about it. Mom calls it good genes. I call it no boobs, and let's face it, having no boobs in high school is a genuine handicap. Once I'm dressed and I've blown out and flat ironed my long brown hair into submission I head back to my room, to find Logan staring out the window.

"Something interesting?" I ask, tossing the damp yellow towel across my chair.

He doesn't turn to look at me.

"I'm just bored. I never realized how boring being dead could be." He sighs deeply, his shoulders slumping as he exhales. "Still, it could be worse."

"Worse than being dead?"

He glances over his shoulder, his blue eyes piercing from across the room. "I could be dead and alone. At least I have you."

I feel a blush creep up my neck and I try to shrug it off. "Yeah, I'm sure you're just dying to hang out with me." Then I force a weak chuckle.

"I mean it, Zoe." He turns, walking toward me slowly, stopping just a few inches away. My heart skips in my chest. Even dead he's the most beautiful boy I've ever seen. From the sharp slope of his nose to the curve of his jaw, from his broad shoulders to his dirty blonde hair that is perfect-messy in the way only movie stars seem to be able to achieve.

"If I didn't have you to talk to—if you couldn't see me—I'd have gone crazy days ago." He reaches out and for a second, and in an idiotic, unrealistic heartbeat in time, I think he's going to touch my face. But before he gets close he drops his hand to his side and the corners of his mouth turn up just a little.

At which point I realize that I'm standing there like a moron.

"Maybe I should start a business." I fan out my hands in front of me. "Zoe Reed. Therapist to the dead."

"You could have business cards with coffins on them."

I snap my fingers, "And my tag line will be, *Just because you're dead doesn't mean you're not crazy.*"

He laughs and it rolls through the room and across my skin like a cold breeze. I shudder and grab a light denim jacket from my closet.

"What's first on the agenda today, General?"

He points to my phone. "First text Carlos about taking you shopping."

I stand up tall and salute him. "Yes sir."

As I'm texting, Logan goes over and starts looking through my closet.

"Carlos has one thing right. You are entering a combat zone. You need a first day battle outfit."

"Ooh, leather and stilettos?"

He looks over his shoulder, frowning.

"The point is to make you look less like…"

"Me?"

"Like you might rip someone in half just for saying hello."

I put a hand on my hip. "So no leather then."

"No. I'm thinking a dress. Something feminine."

Oh sure. Pick the one thing I don't own.

My phone vibrates. "Ok, Carlos is in, and judging by the amount of happy faces in this text, he's a little excited."

It vibrates again.

"He wants to take me to Potomac Mills, to the designer outlets."

"So?"

"And how shall I pay for those expensive garments? With my good looks and winning personality?"

He frowns. I take a deep breath and go to my dresser, pulling open the top drawer. Pushing aside the underwear I grab the small black wallet.

"I didn't want to have to do this." I open the

billfold and remove the one lonely card from the slot.

"What's that?"

"My debit card to my college fund." I clutch it tightly. What little inheritance I'd received from my dad's insurance policy went into this account. I've never used a penny of it, not until now. It always felt like blood money.

"Do you have enough?" he asks.

I glare at him.

"You owe me for this, Logan. Big time. When you get up there, you had better give me a damn good recommendation. I mean it."

He grins, "Deal."

Twenty minutes later Carlos arrives, blasting the horn from the driveway. Mom is gone when I walk out the door. She probably had to make a grocery run for her famous rhubarb pie ingredients.

"Hey Zoe," Carlos offers with way too much enthusiasm for this hour of the morning. He hands me a tall coffee which I accept gratefully. Logan appears in the back seat. I sigh. I hadn't wanted him to go with us but he refused to be left behind. His death was very boring apparently. Even after I'd suggested he chill out in the girl's locker room at the gym he refused to be anywhere but attached to my hip. I just hope I don't forget Carlos can't see or hear him and start talking to 'myself'.

It's a long ride from my small town to the Outlet Mall in Potomac Mills and Carlos talks the whole way. Most of the discussion is about his upcoming date, the first he's had since the firmly-in-the-closet-quarterback fiasco of sophomore year. I try to be pleasantly interested and encouraging, and ignore Logan who is singing along with the radio at the top of his lungs. Digging through my purse I find my small bottle of pills and pop two in my mouth.

"I'm sorry, are you getting a migraine sweetheart?" Carlos asks, patting me on the knee.

"It's not you," I say honestly and smile.

Logan huffs in the back seat and leans forward, poking his head between us.

"Consider this payback for all the rude names you've called me in the last few days."

. I sigh.

"So, where to first?" Carlos asks as we finally pull into the parking lot.

I have no idea where to begin. There must be fifty stores, all trendy boutiques I've never heard of.

"Left to right?" I offer weakly.

Carlos shakes his head. "No, what sort of clothes are you thinking?"

Logan yells in my ear but I ignore him.

"I need something," I pause, waiting for Logan to shut up before I continue. "Feminine."

For a brief second I think Carlos is going to wet himself with excitement. He reaches across the car and pulls me into a bone crushing hug.

I pat his back and he releases me.

"What was that for?" I ask.

He wipes a pretend tear from his eye. "My baby

girl is growing up."

I slug him in the arm.

"I'm serious Zoe. I've been waiting for you to dress like a girl for three years."

I roll my eyes and step out of the car.

"Well, your wait is over."

I see Logan climbing out of the car behind me so I slam the door on him. He looks up at me half of him still in the car, half of him hanging out the door.

"Hey. That wasn't very nice."

I smile and let Carlos take me by the arm and lead me to the first boutique.

Three hours and eight hundred dollars later I officially have more bags than I can carry. Still, Carlos insists on one more shop. Exhausted and feeling like I've burned a hole in my poor credit card I protest, but he makes a pouty puppy face and I relent.

"Let him have his fun," Logan advises.

"I am," I mutter under my breath as we enter the last store. All three of us come to a complete stop two steps in. Across the room, on a rack near the dressing room, hangs the most beautiful red dress I've ever seen.

Carlos grabs me by the arm and points to it.

"That one."

I shuffle my bags over to him. The sales woman, more than happy to help after seeing my haul from the other stores, puts me in a dressing room. It looks even better on, if that's possible. It's a halter cut red sundress that drapes in delicate folds from the waist. There's a line of tiny woven designs around the hem which hits me at just mid-thigh. It has a 1950's vibe without looking costume-ish. And looking at myself in the mirror, for the first time I can see why Carlos thinks I'm pretty. I twist my long brown hair up the back of my neck experimentally. It's perfect. This is my war dress.

And I feel ready for battle.

"I want to see it," Carlos whines from outside.

Not patient enough to wait, Logan slips just his head through the door making me jump.

"Wow," he says, looking me over in a way that makes blood rush to my cheeks.

"Out of the dressing room, perv." I whisper before stepping out to show Carlos.

He grins proudly and motions for me to spin around.

"It's stunning. You're stunning."

"Good," I say looking over myself in the bi-fold mirrors outside the dressing area. I run my hands down the bodice area. This dress even gives me the illusion of having boobs. It's a freaking miracle dress. Reaching down I grab the price tag and almost lose my balance. This dress is over five hundred dollars. I glance up and see Logan watching me from the door to my dressing room. He looks...

Enchanted.

"This better work," I mumble more to myself than anyone else.

"What was that?" the overly eager cashier asks.

I take a deep breath. "I said, I'll take it."

Six

I FALL ASLEEP ON THE WAY HOME and at some point Logan vanishes. By the time I get home it's growing dark and I feel like I've been hit by a truck. Who knew shopping could be so much work?

Carlos helps me get the bags in before skipping off to gloat about his victory on his vlog. I'm sure he is going to tell the whole world about our little adventure. As soon as it's online I watch, but there's only a brief mention of the day's shopping marathon. It's mostly about the movie he saw last week, and of course, about the latest fashion blogs. I click off my computer and heat up some left over soup for dinner. I'm curled up on the sofa when mom gets home, quickly changes, then heads off to work the graveyard shift. I fall asleep watching SyFy not long after that.

"Hey, hey," Logan calls.

I crack one eye open and he's sitting beside me on the couch.

"Good, you're awake."

I flip him off.

"What time is it?"

He glances over his shoulder, "Um…two twenty."

"I hate you."

"I know," he smiles.

Reluctantly I sit up and flick the TV off, shuffling to my room like a zombie.

"Whoa, where are you going?"

"Bed. You know, where you go to sleep."

He moves in front of me to cut me off, but I'm so tired I just step right through him.

"Hey," he protests and follows me to my room.

I shut the door on him, as if that's going to keep him out.

As expected he slides through the door just as I fall into bed.

"Seriously? I come to bring you good news and this is how you treat me?"

I close my eyes. "You're still here. The news can't be that good."

He sits on the edge of my bed and though I don't see it. I can sort of feel it, kind of the way you can feel when someone is watching you.

"Fine." I sit up, pulling my thick green blanket around me to ward off his chill. "What is your news?"

"I was just at Bruno's house—"

"Stalker."

"Anyway. He was talking about having to be at lacrosse tryouts tomorrow. They are doing it before school starts this year."

I yawn. "This is good news how?"

"Well, they are going to be announcing who is taking my place as team captain. And I'm sure it's going to be Bruno. The guys love him."

I wave my hand, "Again, this matters to me because…?"

"Because he was talking to Zach about how lucky Zach is to have his girlfriend coming to support him. It's sort of a tradition that the girls come and watch tryouts, good luck and all."

"Really?"

He nods excitedly. "And since Bruno doesn't have a girlfriend, if you were to happen to be there, I dunno maybe working on something for the newspaper or the student council, you do that stuff right?"

I nod.

"Well, if you were there to wish him luck, maybe stick around and congratulate him after he makes captain…"

I sigh. I'm still not following his train of thought.

"Well, I'm sure he'll ask you out. He already likes you and—"

"Wait, all I have to do to get him to ask me out is show up at practice? Is he totally desperate?"

Logan sits back, rolling his eyes. "No Zoe. He's a guy. We really aren't complicated creatures. When a pretty girl shows interest, maybe drops a few compliments, we are like human putty."

Ah I see now. "So feed his ego a little."

"Exactly."

I'm trying to decide how to handle this new bit of information. I eyeball the red dress hanging on my door.

"Fine. But I'm not going to giggle and bat my eyelashes like a freaking idiot."

He lowers his chin, looking at me seriously.

"One other thing you should do."

"What?"

"Try to go five minutes without insulting anyone, okay?"

Five minutes with no insults? That might actually kill me.

He chuckles at my reaction.

"You can do it. You do it with Carlos all the time."

I swallow. Carlos is different. He's like…family.

"No promises. Now get out of my bed so I can sleep."

Logan gets up and heads for the chair.

"No, like out of my room."

He looks back at me, his eyes sad.

"I don't really have anywhere else to go. My parents packed up my room today. It's just boxes now."

And in that moment, I feel like the biggest bitch alive.

"Okay." I say, lying back down. Then, as I watch him fold himself into my chair, I realize he's going to spend all night there. Just like that, staring off into the dark. Reaching over I grab the tiny remote off my night stand and flick the TV on.

"What channel?"

He looks up appreciatively. "Try USA. They have decent shows usually."

I set the remote back down, roll over so my back is to the TV and curl up in a ball, pulling the covers over my head.

The light is already streaming in my window when I finally stretch and sit up in bed. Logan is gone, but probably not for long. I'm halfway through a bowl of Cheerios by the time he reappears.

"Sleep okay?" he asks sitting beside me at the kitchen table.

I answer with my mouth full. "Yep. Thanks."

"Good. You needed your beauty sleep."

I frown around my spoon. "What are you trying to say?"

He holds up his hands in surrender.

"Nothing. I meant nothing. You look quite rejuvenated today. That's all."

He's probably right. I didn't have any bad dreams last night, for the first time in as long as I can remember. Though I hate to admit it, I think having him there helped. Made me feel…safe somehow. Which is stupid because, well, it's Logan.

"What time are tryouts today?"

"Four," he answers, eyeballing my bowl.

"Hungry?"

He cocks his head to the side. "I don't know. I can't tell if I'm actually hungry, or if I'm just remembering what it feels like to be hungry."

I pick a cheerio out of the bowl and motion for him to open his mouth, which he does. I toss the tiny O and it lands right in his mouth, then flies out the back of his head and sticks to the wall behind him.

He turns to look at it and we both burst into hysterical laughter until my sides hurt and I can't breathe.

Finally we calm ourselves and he waits in the bedroom while I shower and dress. I choose a soft yellow skirt and my new black ballet flats. Logan picks out a deep green ruffled shirt which I slide on over my yellow tank top. I carefully pull my hair back into a loose, casual braid. When I'm done, I stare at myself in the mirror.

"Wow, invasion of the body snatchers," I murmur.

"You look great," Logan assures me.

I have to admit, I do look pretty good. It's not what I'm used to, but it isn't bad either. As a matter of fact, I really like the new look. For the insane amounts of cash I dropped, I sure as hell better.

"So," I begin hesitantly. "I was thinking maybe we should go to The Tower."

He folds his arms across his chest, his face tightening into a scowl.

"Yeah. I've been thinking the same thing. Maybe

I can jog my memory."

I nod. The old Apple Mountain Radio Tower is a solid half hour drive into the woods. I've only been once but I remember it not being terribly hard to get to. It used to be a pretty popular party spot, but a few years back some drunk kid wandered off and got attacked by a mountain lion. Since then, few people go up there. The Tower is mostly overgrown with brush now, and the old foot bridge is in tatters with lots of missing boards and stuff. I'd gone up with a volunteer group last year to put up warning signs and rope off the entrance to the bridge. Part of my community service for my college application. The Tower would be the perfect place to kill someone.

"Any idea why you might go up there?" I ask, wondering if Logan made frequent visits to the place.

He rubs the side of his face. "Well, Kaylee and I used to drive up there sometimes. You know. To be alone."

I should have guessed.

"But when we went up together, we always took her Jeep. I didn't want to scratch up my car," He adds thoughtfully.

"That's weird. You sure you never went up there alone? Or with anyone else?"

"Not that I remember. Why?"

I walk out to the garage and dig through the recycle bin. There, buried under a week's worth of newspaper, is what I'm looking for. I pull it out and bring it inside, holding up the front page. There, in grainy black and white, is a photo of police standing around the entrance to the bridge, wrapping it with crime scene tape. And in the upper left corner, is the unmistakable hood of Logan's new Dodge Charger, complete with the medal from last year's Lacrosse championship hanging from his rear view mirror.

"Because they found your car at the scene. When you went missing, they used the low jack on your car to find you. I remember reading about it."

He leans forward, examining the image. Then he shakes his head.

"I just don't remember."

"It's okay," I say, folding up the paper and stuffing it in my purse. "Let's go have a look. Maybe something will jog your memory."

I grab my keys off the counter and we head out to my car. As soon as the garage door opens he looks over his shoulder and almost screams.

"Wait."

I slam on the brakes and follow his gaze. I don't see anything but empty sidewalk behind us.

"What?"

For a second I'm afraid I've almost hit Brim or something terrible.

He blinks, rubs his eyes with his thumbs, then looks back again.

"I thought I saw something."

My eyes widen. He shakes his head.

"Never mind. It's nothing."

"You sure?"

He nods, not looking entirely convinced. I grab my sunglasses off the console and slip them over my eyes as I drop it back in reverse and pull out. Logan doesn't say anything the whole way up the mountain except occasionally pointing me in the right direction when I come to a fork in the road. He just rests his head against the window and stares off. I'm busy looking at him and not paying attention to the increasingly bumpy dirt road and I hit a rut, making the car jump and Logan's head bounces off the glass with a thud.

"Ouch," he mutters, rubbing his forehead. I slam on the breaks, reach out and try to touch him, but my hand passes right through feeling nothing but cold air where he should be.

"What are you doing?" he demands, looking at me like I've totally lost my mind.

"You felt that."

"Yeah, so?"

"So? You felt that. Like, you *felt* it."

His face falls into a surprised expression. "Oh, yeah I did." He experimentally raises a clenched fist and tries to tap on the window, but just passes through it. "Weird. I wonder why."

I pucker my mouth and resume the drive. A vague theory is forming in my head, but now is not the time to test it. A few more yards and I pull into a narrow gravel parking area and stop the car. Climbing out, I can see the bright sun directly overhead, but I can't see The Tower. The trees are taller and fuller than I remember and I have no idea which way to go from here.

Curse my naturally poor sense of direction.

Logan steps out of the car and walks forward. "This way."

He walks through the trees without hesitation. I however, have to push through the foliage like I'm on safari.

"Why do I never have a good machete when I need one?" I mutter, making Logan chuckle ahead of me.

Soon I can hear the rushing water of the river, though it's still a few hundred yards before I can see it. Then, suddenly, the trees are behind us and the tall iron tower appears in the middle of the woods. There are bushes and tall grass growing along the bottom, with vines of ivy climbing up its monstrous legs. The once silver metal has corroded to a rusty patina and in places it's covered with a living carpet of spongy looking green moss.

It's beautiful, in a very ominous, terrifying way.

"Hold on." I scan the area, walking toward the still taped off bridge. "In the picture, your car was…" I find the matted down grass and follow it to the recent tire tracks. "here. Why in the world would you have driven through the brush, tearing up the paint on your car, instead of just parking over in the gravel?"

I look up, but he's staring over at the bridge. The metal cables look mostly intact and a bit rusty, but the wooden boards are old and splintered, just as I remembered.

"I have no idea," Logan says, not looking at me.

I don't see anything lying on the ground as I scan the area. Anything Logan might have left here was probably taken as evidence by the police.

"I'm going to climb up and see if I can spot anything from the top," I say not waiting for a response. Pushing my way through the wild tangle of leaves and branches I find the rungs of the ladder attached to the side of the tower. I grab ahold of the ladder and cry out. A sliver of metal is poking out and it has sliced into the tender skin of my palm, causing me to jerk my hand away. I hiss, stopping to check it out.

"You alright?" Logan asks, making his way over to me.

I cuss colorfully. "I'm fine. It's not deep."

It just stings like a son of a bitch.

Careful to avoid the sharp protrusion I climb up the first few rungs. The ladder echoes with metallic clangs as my shoes touch the bars. I look down and see Logan staring up at me.

Right up my skirt.

"Hey," I call, grabbing my skirt and tucking it between my legs in the back.

He rolls his eyes. "I'm not looking up your skirt Zoe."

"Whatever perv. Go check out the bridge."

"I'm not going on the bridge," he says folding his arms across his chest.

I glare down. "Are you kidding me? You're already

dead. What's the worst that could possibly happen?"

He doesn't move. I growl.

"Fine, you insecure butt clown. Just stand there and let me do all the work."

I hear him mutter something rude and head for the bridge. As soon as I'm confident he's not staring at my underwear I continue to climb. About halfway up, the ladder opens into an internal staircase inside the skeletal tower. I step carefully onto the diamond steel platform and grab the rail with my uncut hand. Ascending the stairs with greater confidence I make my way to the top of the tower. The metal roof is low and I wonder briefly how they used to get equipment up here at all. The last platform is bare except for the steel railing all the way around and the long rails holding the roof up. Leaning over the railing I can see for miles. Mountains hover in the distance. I can see not just the river closest to me, but far down stream where the two rivers merge.

"See anything?" Logan calls, shielding his hand with his eyes as he looks up at me.

"Nope. You?"

"Nothing."

I turn around to head down when I feel something under my foot. I think it might be a pebble, but when I look down I see a delicate silver chain sticking out under my shoe. Reaching down I pick up the broken chain and the small silver pendant that has broken off. It's a mangled silver leaf.

I hurry down the ladder and show the necklace

to Logan.

"This was up there. Do you recognize it?"

He stares at it for a second and his face brightens, then falls.

"It's Kaylee's. Or it was."

"Was?"

He snaps his fingers. "I remember now. She gave it back to me when she dumped me last week."

I straighten, tucking it in my pocket. "Wow. Didn't see that coming."

He looks around. "But that happened at her house. So how did that get here?"

I shrug. "Maybe you brought it when you came?"

"And put it all the way up there?" he asks, giving me a duh stare.

"Good point." He pulls his fingers through his hair.

"I'd forgotten about that. About her breaking up with me."

I jerk my head towards the car and start walking.

"So, what happened?" I ask, morbidly curious. They always seemed like the perfect couple.

He stops at the car door before answering. "I accused her of cheating on me. I found something...a text on her phone. Yeah we were at her house and she went to get a snack and left her phone. Someone texted her, something about getting rid of me so they could meet up later. I confronted her and she told me..."

I'm completely curious now. "Told you what?"

He clears his throat, "She told me that she met someone who had his life together. Said she needed someone who could understand her on a more *mature* level. We argued and she took it off and handed it to me."

His expression is distant as he continues.

"And I left." He snaps his fingers, "But before I did, I hung it inside her car, from the mirror."

"So she had it when you died?"

He sighs. "Maybe. I don't remember anything after that."

I nod, leaning against the car door and patting the roof. "Yeah, but you're remembering, which is good. It means you *can* remember. I'm sure it'll all start coming back now."

He leans forward, moving through the car into the seat. "I hope you're right."

I open the door and climb in, sticking the key in the ignition. "It means something else too."

He looks at me curiously.

I sigh. "It means I need to figure out a way to talk to Kaylee."

Seven

WE HIT A DRIVE THROUGH on the way home, then spend the rest of the day in my room brainstorming ways I can approach Kaylee about Logan's death. And their break up. And the necklace. After two hours, the best thing we come up with is a story about aliens and secret government agencies experimenting on High School students.

Deciding not to waste a trip to the school, I text a few other student council members and put together an impromptu meeting right before tryouts. With a careful application of lip gloss and a quick re-braid to get out the random twigs and leaves stuck in my hair from my earlier adventure, I pull the necklace out of my skirt pocket and put it on top of my dresser. I wash the dry blood off of my hand, which is throbbing, and put a band-aid over it.

Logan looks me over. "Okay, are you ready for this?"

I nod. Grabbing my notebook and a pencil I head for the car.

"I'll be right here in case you need any help," Logan assures me on the way.

I snort. "What are you going to do? Give him hypothermia?"

He puts a hand to his chest, pretending to be hurt. "I am not without skills."

I glance over at him, then back to the road. "Oh really? Name three."

He's quiet for a second, and then pouts.

"That's cold, Zoe."

I humph. That's what I thought.

We pull into the parking lot and I see Bruno's old black truck. He's probably the only one of Logan's friends who isn't sporting a shiny new ride. I pull up beside it and park just as Bruno crawls out of the back, his stick and pads in hand.

Taking a deep breath I glance across at Logan who gives me an enthusiastic smile and two thumbs up.

"Just, keep quiet," I mutter to him as I open my door.

Rounding the car, I see that Bruno is watching me and I can't fight back the grin on my face.

"Hey," I offer coyly. "What's going on?"

His eyes widen just a little, like he's shocked that I'm talking to him. He actually does a quick glance to each side to make sure there isn't someone behind him. Then he relaxes.

"Hi Zoe." He stumbles just a little, his stick falling out of his meaty hand. We both lean over to pick it up, but I get there first. He stands up, blushing a fierce red as I stuff it under his arm.

"Are you guys starting practices already?"

I start walking toward the school and he falls in step beside me, grinning like a little puppy.

"Um, yeah. No. Sort of." He clears his throat. "It's tryouts. We have to break in a few new players. And uh…" he pauses for a few seconds before continuing. "We need to choose a new team captain."

There's just enough of a breeze that my loose braid is falling apart, strands blowing wildly. I try to tuck them behind my ears. In the corner of my eye I see Bruno shake his head to move the dark hair falling in over his blue eyes. He really is kind of adorable, I realize. I suppose I never really looked that closely before, but now I see the dimple in his chin that matches the ones in his cheeks, the perfect arc of his nose, even the impossibly long, thick eyelashes only boys are ever blessed with.

"I hear you're a shoe in for Captain."

His step falters. "Really?"

I nod.

"Who told you that?"

I lower my chin and smile, hoping it looks coy instead of nervous as a sliver of panic slices into my belly. Beside me Logan slaps himself in the forehead.

"Well," I offer, changing the subject, "I have a student council meeting."

"Offer to catch up with him after," Logan instructs from my other side.

"Maybe I'll see you later?"

We reach the doors and Bruno reaches out, pulling the door open for me.

"That would be great." He blushes again and it's really hard not to chuckle. I never in a million years would have guessed he could be so…sappy.

I wave and turn down the hall opposite us as he keeps going straight, toward the locker room.

"Slow down." Logan demands.

I slow my pace and hear Bruno call from behind me.

"Hey Zoe?"

I turn slowly, crossing my ankles and folding my hands behind my back. "Yes?"

"You wanna hang out later?"

I look down at my feet, waiting for instructions from Logan. Do I say no? Play hard to get? God, I suck at flirting.

"Say yes," Logan whispers impatiently.

I look back up and nod, "Yeah. I'd like that. See you after tryouts?"

Bruno grins widely and a ripple of guilt washes over me. As he turns away I whisper out the side of my mouth to Logan.

"He really does like me."

Logan frowns and shakes his head.

"What?" I demand, watching the expression on his face.

"You are gonna eat that poor guy alive."

I'm not sure how to take that so I just turn and head for the library and my meeting.

Stepping through the wooden doors is like stepping through time. The scent of old books, stale and crisp, hangs thick in the air. I pause, letting the memory of my first time here wash over me. Freshmen year, just paroled from a year trapped in home-school, I walked through these doors and into a world like nothing I expected. It wasn't scary, just bigger than I expected. High school is like a city unto itself, complete with celebrities, despots, and nameless faces that never really leave their mark. From my first friendless day I resigned myself to virtual obscurity. Even joining student council and a half dozen other clubs hadn't increased my social stock. Still, they look good on college applications so I kept going, kept waiting for my time to shine. At one of the large round tables my classmates sit chatting happily.

Peter Lawton, class president and obligatory math nerd catches sight of me and waves. The others turn and stare for a second before smiling and waving me over. Lucy Parsons, a vibrant red-haired junior leaps out of her seat and tosses her arms around me, squeezing. I pat her back lightly. I have never been much of a hugger.

She pulls back, sliding her hands down my arms.

"You look amazing!"

I murmur thanks and let her lead me over to the table. Carson, our vice president, and one of the few people I talk to on a regular basis on account of being lab partners last year, stands and hugs me quickly. His one-time girlfriend Leena sits across the table from him with her legs crossed, flicking her flip flops with her toes. She nods, but doesn't look overly thrilled to be here. I understand why. Her new boyfriend is on the Lacrosse team and she would probably much rather be out there watching him than in here with her ex.

Carson pulls out my chair—something he's never done in the year I've known him—and I take a seat, pulling a black spiral notebook out of my bag.

"Hey guys. Thanks for meeting up."

Lucy sits forward, taking a sip from a very tall, very whipped creamed coffee drink. Her wide eyes and overall jitteriness is almost comical.

"Hey, I'm so excited to meet up! I can't wait for this year, so many fun things going on! We have prom and Homecoming and the decade dances—"

Leena silences her. "Yeah. That's great. Can we get to the point? Some of us have lives?"

I lower my chin and stare at her. This is the point where I normally call Leena a worthless waste of skin bobble head and tell her to leave. She's staring at me like she expects the insult and has prepared some kind of clever comeback. I glance over, looking for Logan but he's gone.

Shame. He's going to miss this.

"I understand Leena, and I'm sorry to pull you away. I just wanted to get together and figure out what our schedules are like, when we can schedule our regular meetings, and to set the date and theme for Homecoming so I can get the Dance Committee going on it."

Leena frowns. Yep, she had some snappy retort planned and I'd ruined her surprise. Poor Leena.

She finally flicks her long brown hair over her shoulder. "Oh. Okay. Well, I have Cheer every day except Friday until six, but I could do after six or right after school on non-game Fridays.

I make a note in my spiral then look over to Carson. He's staring at me. When I look over, he blinks.

"Oh, yeah Fridays are out for me. But I get out of practice at six on Monday, so I could do that."

"Does that work for you, Pete?" I ask.

He's looking at his phone, probably checking his calendar.

"No good. I Dungeon Master for RPG club on Monday."

Lucy pipes up. "What about before school?"

The rest of the table groans.

I pat her hand gently.

"Mornings are a good idea, but that's a little too early for the ones who wear themselves out at practice every night." I look around the table. Leena has sat back in her seat and folded her arms under her chest. She's grinning at me like she knows I'm up to something. "What if we meet up on the first Saturday of the month at Pablo's coffee at ten am?"

"Do you think that's enough time? Once a month?" Pete asks, his eyebrows furrowing behind his big glasses.

"I think it'll be fine. And we can always keep in

touch via email and text for things that can't wait." I offer.

Lucy claps excitedly. "I love that idea."

I'm just about to make a snide remark about her excitability level but thankfully Leena does it for me.

"Lucy, switch to decaf. Seriously. Before you explode."

I grin. Why aren't Leena and I friends again? Then she turns to me, her voice dripping with venom and I remember.

"Fine. But my breakfast comes out of the budget. No way am I paying to share a meal with you guys."

I look over at Pete who nods.

"Okay then. We will meet again next Saturday at ten am." I make another note. "Now we just need to decide on the date and theme for Homecoming. Ideas?"

This time it's Carson who is tapping away on his phone.

"First home game of the season is October 1st, Saturday night."

"So we plan the dance for Friday?" I ask and they all agree.

"I think we should do a sports theme," Carson says, smacking his hand on the table like a gavel.

"Noooooo," Lucy says flatly.

"I agree with Lucy, for once," Leena adds.

"What about a dragon theme?" Peter suggests. Leena balls up a piece of paper and throws it at his head, knocking his glasses askew.

"Forget it elf-boy."

"I like the idea of a fairy tale theme," Lucy says dreamily.

Visions of pink tutus dance in my head and I shudder.

"Do you have any suggestions Leena?" I ask. She eyeballs me suspiciously then leans forward.

"What about a Venetian Masked Ball?"

As soon as she says it, I'm in. It sounds cool and unique and something we haven't done before. I can tell from his expression that Carson isn't sold, so I speak up.

"So classy and sleek. Guys look all 007 with those cool black masks, girls in lace and satin. I like it."

I may not know much about guys, but I do know that the slightest mention of James Bond can convince them that anything is a good idea.

"Vote?" Pete says. "All in favor of Leena's idea raise your hand."

Everyone but him raises their hand. He sighs. "Motion passed."

Lucy claps again.

"Great, I'll make the announcement to the Dance Committee and let the principal know."

"Any other business?" Pete asks before slamming his notebook closed. "Then meeting adjourned. See you guys next weekend."

Leena dashes off, but the others mill around just a bit. Peter puts his hand on my shoulder as he's leaving. "Good meeting, madam secretary."

I tilt my head in thanks. He's right. It's the

first time we got through a whole meeting without me insulting someone or Leena losing her shit and making Lucy cry or Carson getting distracted by his phone and tuning out completely.

Diplomacy. Who knew?

Carson walks over to the stacks, looking for a book.

"That was amazing," Lucy says, scooping up her bag.

"What?" I ask.

"You. You just walked in and owned the place. I've never seen you look so good."

I shrug, tugging at the hem of my skirt. "Thanks. It's new."

She leans over further, her face really setting off my personal space alarms.

"It's not the clothes Zoe. It's you, how you carried yourself today. I've never seen you look so confident." She sits back, looking day-dreamy, like she might burst out in a sonnet or something. "It's like you've been this weird, angry caterpillar. But now you're a kind, lovely butterfly."

That's too much. I literally throw up in my mouth a little. Forcing a smile I pat her hand.

"Thanks Lucy."

She grins and leaves me to gather the last of my things and throw away the empty drink cup she left behind. I turn and nearly barrel into Carson.

"She's right. You were awesome today."

"Thanks," I murmur and step around him, tossing

the cup in the trash and sliding my purse onto my shoulder.

I leave and he jogs to catch up with me. "So, who do you have for Advanced Bio this year?"

I pause, trying to recall the schedule I'd gotten in the mail only last week. "Um, Wells, I think. You?"

"I have Wells too. Fifth period?"

"Yep."

He grins, running his hand through the back of his light blonde hair. "So, do you wanna be lab partners again?"

I freeze. Last year we'd been paired up in class, quite unwillingly as I recall. Only after a few months had he warmed up enough to talk to me outside of class. Yet here he is, asking me to partner up again. I'm far from a genius, but I hold my own in all my AP classes, so of course he'd want me for a partner.

So why does it feel like he's asking me on a date?

"Yeah. Sure."

"Cool."

We wave goodbye and he heads off. I make my way through the empty school toward the practice field. I open the door to the bright daylight and see that Logan is standing on the sidelines, watching. The expression on his face is serene. I walk up next to him and pull the phone from my pocket, holding it to my ear.

"What are you doing?"

I sigh. "I'm pretending to talk on my phone so if anyone sees me here with my lips moving they just think

I'm taking a call."

"Oh. Good idea."

"I know."

He claps as Bruno saves a particularly nasty looking goal.

"You okay?" I ask, watching as his face goes from proud to sad. His smile slips and he drops his hands.

"Nope. Not even a little."

A pang of grief drives into my heart like a spike. My hand twitches, the instinct to reach over and take his hand is so strong I barely catch myself. Then I laugh dryly.

"What's funny?" He asks, his voice irritated.

I shake my head. "I was just wishing I could hug you or something."

He stares at me for a second, then he laughs too. "Probably not a good idea. You don't want to look like a crazy person in front of all those witnesses." He jerks his head, indicating the small crowd sitting on the metal bleachers.

Fair enough.

I put my phone away and cross the sidelines, taking a seat on the lower bleacher. Leena sits down, scooting beside me.

"Since when do you watch practices?"

"I'm meeting up with Bruno after," I say, squinting against the bright sunlight.

I can feel her appraising me. "You know, I always thought you had a thing for Carson."

"Carson? No. No way."

She snorts, "You say that like he's beneath you."

I take a deep breath, trying to actually consider my words before they fly out of my mouth.

"No, it's not that. It's just that Carson is a friend. Besides, he was totally head over heels for you." There. Maybe a little flattery will appease the beast.

She flips her hair, exposing the long line of her neck. "Well, that's over now. So, are you going after him?"

That surprises me enough that I turn to her. "No. I'm not."

She looks at me, weighing my words. "Okay. Not that I care but, you know."

No. I have no idea why she's trying to get into a pissing match over a guy she's not even seeing anymore. I almost say as much too, but she cuts me off before I can.

"I still care about him. And the way you walked into the room today, it was like you were a tiger on the prowl."

I make a face and she rolls her eyes.

"Trust me, I've perfected that strut over the years. It's the *I'm a hot piece of woman and every male in this room is going to want me* walk."

I shake my head. "Well, that's not what I was going for."

She leans back like she's sunbathing. "I get that now. You really don't know what your little sashay did to those poor helpless boys. But you better learn, and quick. Before you have more guys barking up your tree than you can handle."

She lowers her head, "And do me a favor, keep Carson in the friend zone, okay?"

I'm tempted to tell her exactly what I think of her weird, bullshit request, but from the corner of my eye I see Bruno watching so I just smile and nod.

She nudges me. "Cool. You know, maybe we should hang out sometime."

"That sounds great." I almost choke on the words.

Turning back to Bruno I see that tryouts are winding down.

"Wave at him and smile," Logan demands. He's sitting behind Leena, staring down her shirt.

Obeying, I wave as subtly as I can, making Bruno break into a grin like nothing I've ever seen. You'd have thought I just gave him a million dollars and the key to my chastity belt.

"You're a natural," Leena says, sounding remarkably pleased, probably glad I'm flirting with Bruno and not Carson. She stands up, wiping off the butt of her short white shorts with a seductive wiggle and heads over to the field where the team has gathered in a large bunch while Coach Mason makes announcements.

Mr. Mason is also the Advanced Calculus teacher and by far the hottest teacher in the world. He kind of reminds me of Captain America. All muscles and boyish grins. He even does the perfect comb to the side hair thing. Basically, he is the reason our school has such a high number of females in advanced math classes. At the end of every year he has a big pool party at his house for the graduating seniors. I'm secure enough to admit that I really hope to score an invitation this year, if, for no other reason than to ogle him in a pair of board shorts.

He says something and the team cheers and claps.

"They just named him captain." Logan says from behind me.

I clap as Bruno stands and takes over the rest of the meeting. I can't hear his words, but at the end everyone cheers and heads for the locker room. Everyone except the guys with girlfriends in the stands—and Bruno.

I climb down and meet him half way. Beside me, Leena takes a run and a flying leap into the hands of her tall, sweaty boyfriend Daryl.

"So," Bruno says, blushing, "They made me captain."

I smile warmly. "I told you they would."

"I...probably need a shower. Do you want to hang out or meet up somewhere?"

Beside me I can hear Leena and Daryl making out loud and wet. I almost gag.

"Why don't we meet up?"

He nods. "James Creek Park?"

I know the place, it's not far from the school, across from Starbucks.

"Cool."

"Offer to bring food." Logan says.

"Um, how about I drive through somewhere and grab some sandwiches?"

His eyes light up like a tree on Christmas freaking

morning.

"That'd be great."

I wave goodbye and head for my car. I glance around, making sure no one is in earshot.

"Why am I bringing food?" I ask Logan who is trailing behind me.

"It's a guy thing. You offer to feed us, and we will agree to just about anything."

I laugh.

"No really, it's a psychological thing. You offer a guy food and he feels like you are taking care of his needs, like it shows you care. Psychology 101."

I stop outside my car door.

"So the way to a man's heart really is through his stomach?"

Logan chuckles. "Basically. Though there are other parts that will get you there too."

I roll my eyes, get in, and start the car. "Great."

Eight

SOMEHOW BRUNO MANAGES to get to the park before me. Probably due to the fact that the drive through worker at the SandWitch was a total moron who couldn't get my order straight until I finally wrote it out for him. It also didn't help that Logan was in my ear the whole time telling me over and over that Bruno doesn't like onions or tomatoes.

Finally I'd just yelled, "I know. No freaking onions or tomatoes."

The cashier was appalled and a curt, "Yes, I heard you ma'am," crackled through the ancient speaker. I proceeded to slam my head into the steering wheel until my food was ready.

Now, as I pull to a stop beside Bruno's truck, I look at Logan sternly.

"You can't keep talking in my ear like that. It's too distracting."

He raises an eyebrow.

I point, "I mean it Logan, either stay here or stay

quiet."

He makes a lip zipping gesture and I climb out of the car, bag of food in one hand, drink carrier in the other.

Bruno is sitting at a picnic bench, staring at his phone.

"Hey," I call and he looks up, relief flooding his face. He jumps to his feet and rushes over, taking the drinks for me.

"Hey," he says as we walk back to his bench with Logan lagging behind.

Opening the bag I pull out his sandwich and dill pickle potato chips.

"Oh yum. I'm starving."

He unwraps the sandwich and spreads the bread, looking for the innards.

"No tomatoes, no onions, right?" I offer and he grins.

"How did you know?" he asks, reassembling his sandwich and taking a bite.

Oh shit.

I try to play it off with a shrug. Just when I'm afraid he's not going to drop it he smiles at me and I feel the tension leaving my body.

"Fine. Be mysterious," he jokes and takes another bite.

I dig in to my own sandwich, not realizing how hungry I am until I've devoured half the sub in five seconds flat.

"So how was your meeting?" he asks, taking a

drink.

I swallow and set my sandwich down.

"Good. Productive." I grin and take a sip, "I didn't even fight with Leena today."

He chuckles, "So, are you applying for sainthood?"

I nod, "I'm considering a run. We just scheduled the stuff for Homecoming so I can turn it over to the Dance Committee."

He stares at me blankly so I continue.

"We decided on a Venetian masquerade. Very 007, you know. Suave."

"Sounds cool."

"I hope so. The Dance Committee are the ones who really make it happen, all the decorations and stuff. I go in to help sometimes, just with the setup. It's fun to see it all come together."

"So are you going?"

I pause mid sandwich pickup. "To the dance?"

He laughs lightly. "No, to the moon. Yes, to the dance."

I shrug, "I dunno. Probably not. I usually don't."

He balls up his wrapper and dusts the crumbs off the table. "Why not?"

I don't look up when I answer. It's so pathetic I can't even meet his eyes.

"I guess…no one's ever asked me."

"Seriously?"

Great. Now I feel like a total loser. And it's not entirely true, Carlos asked me to be his date last year, but it was a pity ask, and I felt like going with him was no better than taking your cousin to prom, so I declined. I feel the flush rising into my face and I have to physically swallow back the smart ass quip fighting its way out my throat.

I hear Bruno laughing dryly so I dip my head lower.

"Freaking Logan."

"What did you say?" he asks, making my face snap up.

I tilt my head. "I said, 'This is all Logan's fault.'"

"How so?" He looks genuinely confused and I want nothing more than to crawl under a rock somewhere and die. I knew this was a stupid plan and now I'm going to throw Logan under the bus—remorse free.

"It's just that, Logan mentioned that you asked for my phone number once. I never thought much of it since you didn't call, but I saw you today and I thought... Never mind. It's stupid."

He reaches out, covering my hands with his. It's an alien sensation, the physical contact with someone not Mom or Carlos.

"Hey. I did call. Like a dozen times." He takes a deep breath, "But I just kept hanging up."

"Why?"

"Because I was never quite sure what to say to you. You were always so uninterested. I only asked you out today because you seemed so...different. Relaxed."

I nod. He didn't call because he thinks I'm a total

ball-buster. Or at least he did.

"But if I'd known you even wanted to go to those dances, I would have asked you to every single one."

I shake my head in disbelief.

"No really. Just like I'm asking you now. Zoe, will you go to Homecoming with me?"

I suck in a breath. This is happening a lot quicker than I expected.

I narrow my eyes, "You aren't just asking because you feel sorry for me, right?"

He laughs again and it's a deep belly laugh. "Zoe, I promise you, I do not feel sorry for you. If I did you'd probably kick me in the junk."

That's probably true. I grin. "Sure. I'd really like to go to the dance with you."

Now it's his turn to smile. "It's a date."

Out the corner of my eye I see Logan head back to the car with a snort.

Nine

LOGAN ISN'T AROUND MUCH for the next few days, leaving me in relative peace. He shows back up the night before school starts, appearing in my room while I'm on the phone with Carlos, rehashing his most recent date with the guy we are now referring to as Mr. Perfect. Logan just pops in and I nearly jump out of my skin. Wrapping up the convo quickly I put my phone onto charge and curl up in my chair.

"You ready for tomorrow?" he asks coolly.

I shake my head. "That's all I get? You disappear for a week and I get a ready for tomorrow?"

"What do you want me to say?"

"How about starting with where the hell you've been for the last few days. Then work your way into an apology. Groveling wouldn't be out of the question."

He sighs, flopping down on my bed.

"I was around."

I fold my arms and glare. I'm pretty sure if looks could kill, he'd be dead. Again. Deader at least.

"I thought I saw someone."

"Who?"

He pauses, taking a deep breath. "Someone like me."

"Another ghost?"

"Not exactly. Something else. I've seen him a few times. It's like, he's following me."

I sit forward, irritation almost gone.

"What does he want?"

Logan shrugs.

"Did you go looking for him?"

"No. I was trying to lead him away."

"Away from what?"

His head snaps up, "From you, Zoe. I was trying to keep him away from you."

I feel my face soften. Irritation gone.

"Why?"

He looks away, "The thing is, he feels…dangerous. Like he wants to hurt me. Or maybe you. I'm not sure, but he just feels malevolent."

"That's a big word for a jock." I quip, unable to restrain myself.

He rolls his eyes.

"Sorry," I offer with a grin. "I've been holding it in all week, it has to come out somewhere."

He's not amused.

"So is he gone?"

Logan shrugs, "I don't know. But I couldn't stay away any longer."

I smile. "You wanna watch TV? There's a special on the Travel Channel."

He sits up, rubbing his face. I'd say he was exhausted, if he could actually get tired anymore. Maybe even dead people can get emotionally tired. Maybe it's even worse for them.

"Sure. What kind of special?"

I flick on my TV. "Exotic Destinations. My favorite. I keep this list of all the places I want to see after I graduate. Sort of my bucket list."

I cringe as soon as the words are out. "Sorry."

He half smiles, staring at the flickering screen. "No big deal."

"Did you have a bucket list?" I ask out of sheer morbid curiosity.

He nods, "I did actually. Didn't get much done."

"What did you get done?"

He starts counting on his fingers, "Surf in Hawaii, we went there on a family vacation a few years ago, walked on a volcano, also saved a life—"

"Whose?"

"Craig Peterson. Last year we were hanging out and he choked on a piece of popcorn. I gave him the Heimlich."

I pucker my lips. "Cool."

"And I had sex. With an actual girl. That was a big one." He laughs and I reach out to slug him in the arm before I can stop myself.

And I hit him.

He looks at me and I look at him. I slug him again and pass through.

Pulling one leg under me, I prop myself up beside him. "Ok, I think I have this figured out."

His eyes are wide, "Really? That would be nice."

I hold up a finger. "Like in the car. You hit your head, and felt it, because you expected to feel it. It was sort of…instinct."

"And just now—"

"You expected me to make contact. It's like for just a second, you forget you're dead. You *forget* that you can't feel, so you do."

"So how do I control it?"

I frown, "That I don't know. But I bet we can figure it out."

"How?"

I hold out my hands. "I don't know. Let's just sit here and talk and relax. Just like we were."

He settles back, "Okay. I can do that."

I sit back too. "So what didn't you get to do on your list?"

"Well, I always wanted to go to New York City. And I never got to crash a wedding. Or invent something—I always thought I'd invent something. And I was really looking forward to college." He pauses, his face growing dark. "Never fell in love."

I can't hide the surprise in my voice. "Really? What about Kaylee?"

He shakes his head. "She was great, but it was

never like that. It was more a relationship of...physical attraction that faded into convenience. I wasn't even mad when she dumped me. It was more like feeling relieved."

"That's pathetic, truly."

"Yeah, yeah. Make fun of the dead guy. What about you, what's on your list?"

I cock my head to the side. "I want to backpack through Europe. See the pyramids. Fly in a hot air balloon. Swim the English Channel. Learn to scuba dive. Climb a mountain. Stand inside the Parthenon. Learn to speak Chinese ."

"Why Chinese?"

I shrug, "So I can order my food in the proper language?"

He laughs and I join in.

"And fall in love," I add softly.

He reaches over and grabs my hand. I can feel it. Just for a minute before he fades away, but I feel it, and I squeeze.

"See? Like that," I say sadly.

At some point I fall asleep, curled up next to a dead guy, which is just too insane for words. He rouses me around one in the morning, whispering my name in my ear, and I crawl into bed without really waking up. When my alarm goes off in the morning, he's sitting in my chair with his legs draped over one arm, his head resting on the other.

"You know, the only thing worse than being dead? Being dead and having to watch crappy TV because I can't change the channel."

I snort, clicking off my wailing siren. A soft knock at my door makes me jump.

Mom pokes her head in.

"Good morning sweetheart. You excited for your first day of senior year?"

I raise an eyebrow and she chuckles.

"Yeah, I figured as much. How about you and I go grab some breakfast and I'll drop you off today?"

Her voice is so hopeful that it's almost painful to turn down the offer.

"Oh. I'd love to but I um…I'm actually getting a ride today."

"Carlos?"

I look away, fighting back the blush crawling up my neck. "No. His name's Kyle Bruno."

She doesn't speak and when I turn back to look at her, she looks like a deer caught in the headlights.

"Why are you looking at me like that?"

She shakes herself out of it. "I'm just surprised. Is he like…a boyfriend?"

I sigh. "No. Not really."

Truth is, he and I have been talking almost every day for a week, and the fact that we will be walking into school together today pretty much makes him my boyfriend, in that vague, unofficial way.

"But you want him to be?" she presses.

I frown. "I don't know Mom. It's complicated."

Do I like Bruno? Yes. Would I ever have gone out

with him if Logan hadn't asked me to? Probably not. But the more I get to know him, the more I realize he really is a good guy.

"Is he cute?"

I grab the red dress from my closet and fold it over my arm. "You know how you think someone is sort of…I don't know, one way, so you never really look at them or think they are good looking. But then you get to know them, and the more you like their personality, the more attractive they get?"

As soon as I say it, a lump forms in my throat because I realize I'm not just talking about Bruno. Logan is still sitting in my chair, listening intently.

Mom's standing there with her hand over her mouth like she's gonna cry.

I roll my eyes. "Ok, that's it. You get out. I need to get ready."

Walking over, I shoo her back and close my door.

"Rain check on breakfast?" she asks through the door.

I press my head against the wood panel. "Sure Mom."

I turn and Logan is staring at me. "Are you really starting to like Bruno?"

I shrug. "He's hard not to like."

Logan nods in agreement. "Still, just keep your eyes on the prize. I'm not playing matchmaker here. He's just your way into the group. You still have to make everyone else like you. Including Kaylee."

I narrow my eyes, "Speaking of, any tips on that front?"

He holds up his hands in a no clue gesture. I sigh.

"Great," I mutter.

"What? Dudes, I get. But chicks are like puzzles with no corner pieces and no pictures on the box."

I just stare at him.

"What?" he asks defensively.

I point to the window. "Get lost so I can get ready."

He sighs, "I thought we were beyond such trivial concerns. Where is your sense of trust?"

I put a hand on my hip. "The same place my foot's about to be."

He snickers. "Fine. You have ten minutes."

"Twenty."

"Prude."

"Perv."

And he's gone, leaving me holding my new dress and wondering why I miss him so much.

I'm just lacing up my black ankle boots when Logan reappears.

"Bruno just left his house, he'll be here in like five…"

I look up, carefully re-adjusting the waves of brown hair behind my shoulders.

His face has frozen in mid word and it's so comical that I laugh.

"You okay there, Polterdouche?"

"You look like a girl," he stammers.

I promptly flip him off.

"Ah, there's my little princess. So Bruno will be here in five minutes. You know the plan, right?"

I salute him. "Secure an invitation to lunch. Create opportunities to befriend Kaylee. Try not to go all Wookie and rip someone's arms out of socket."

I lift my foot into the air, "And try not to kill myself in these shoes."

He nods, appraising me. "Good. Yeah. Great."

He moves over to the window, staring outside.

"But I need you to do me a favor, Logan."

He looks back over his shoulder, eyebrows furrowing. "What?"

I slide my denim jacket on and grab my messenger bag. "Don't follow me into class, ok. You are just…too distracting."

"Fair enough. I can see how looking at me would be a distraction. I'll walk you into first period, then I'll just wander around until lunch, sound good?"

I look at him, one eyebrow raised in suspicion. He gave in way too easily on that.

"Wandering where?"

He feigns a hurt look. "I'm not going to be hanging out in the girl's locker room if that's what you were thinking."

I'm still not sure I trust the cocky grin on his face but I don't have time to argue because the tell-tale sound of Bruno's truck roars into my driveway. I dart out of my room and stride toward the front door. Mom's sitting at the table.

"Do I get to meet him?" she hollers over her cup of coffee.

"No," I call back with a goodbye wave.

I already have my hand on the knob when the doorbell rings. Pulling my hand back I take a deep breath, lift my chin, and straighten my shoulders.

A quick glance over my shoulder tells me Logan is right beside me. I open the door and Bruno smiles.

"Hey. Are you ready?"

"Yep." I pull the door closed on Logan who floats through with a huff. "Thanks for picking me up."

"Well, you're on the way."

I laugh. "No I'm not. I'm three miles in the opposite direction."

He shrugs, "Still."

Bruno blushes, rushing to my side of the truck and pulling the door open for me.

I mutter, "Thanks," and slide in.

The inside of his truck is spotless, even the beat up carpet under my feet is freshly vacuumed. A little round air freshener hangs from his rear view mirror, right next to his championship lacrosse medal.

The leather dash is worn and faded grey. The old radio has been removed, a fancy new deck installed. It glows red, music gently throbbing through the speakers. I recognize the song. It's one of my favorite bands. The music is upbeat and peppy and I start humming along without thinking.

Bruno slides in and smiles. He's gotten a haircut since the last time I saw him. His dark hair is shorn close to his scalp, too short to comb, but long enough to run his fingers through before grinding into gear.

"I didn't know you liked Matt & Kim. They're one of my favorite bands." I say, carefully crossing my legs.

He raises one shoulder in a half shrug as we drive off. "I know," he says pointedly.

I sit back, a little surprised. "How do you know?"

"I can be mysterious too, you know."

I shake my head softly. "Fair enough."

I ask him about his summer, trying nonchalantly to steer the conversation toward the past few weeks, trying to dig out any info about Logan's missing days. He talks about everything but Logan. I can't blame him really, it's probably sore spot. Still, I need the info.

We pull in and I stare at the front doors. People are milling around, hugging each other and talking. I catch sight of Kaylee and her roving band of followers as they stride into the school like a pack of wolves in high heels.

I suck in a deep breath, deliberately trying to look even more nervous than I feel.

"You okay?" he asks.

I nod once.

"Do you think they will have grief counselors and stuff?"

Last year when some freshman died in a car accident, they had grief counselors stationed in the library for a week. It was weird and disruptive, and basically an excuse to get out of that test you forgot to prepare for or that class you hated.

He sighs. "No. School policy. They don't do that in cases of suicide. Don't want to glamorize it."

That makes my head snap up.

"Suicide?" Logan and I say at the same time, though obviously Bruno can only hear me. "I thought it was an accident?"

He shifts in his seat, looking really uncomfortable.

"That's the word his family put out. But my uncle works for the Sherriff. The official cause of death on the report is suicide."

I can feel my face contort in rage. "That's idiotic. Logan would never do that."

"Damn right," Logan adds from the back seat.

"I know. That's what I told them. But I guess Kaylee had just dumped him, and he took it really hard. Or that's what she said anyway."

I can't stop the words before they fly out of my mouth. "That lying bitch."

I look over and Bruno is grinning.

"Sorry," I say quickly.

"Why?"

I purse my lips together. "I'm trying not to be

quite so…"

"Dickish?" Logan offers.

"Harsh." I say instead. "Carlos keeps telling me I'm abrasive."

"Like steel wool toilet paper," Logan mutters.

I rub my forehead.

"Well, don't be sorry." Bruno offers, nudging me gently. "I like it when you speak your mind. You're so—"

"Bitchy?"

"Honest. And funny. That's why I like you. So just, you know, don't try to change too much. I like you as is. Mouth and all."

I stare at him, not sure what to say.

Wow. I could literally kiss him right now.

I finally decide to take it as a compliment and mumble a weak, "Thanks."

He opens his door, looking back at me before closing it. "Besides, you're right. She is a lying bitch. I mean, Logan wasn't the type of guy to go all emo over a girl." He pauses, "Not even Kaylee."

I glance over at Logan as I get out of the truck. He looks absolutely livid.

"She's lying," Logan says through a clenched jaw.

I nod so he knows I believe him and shut the door.

So the million dollar question is, why would she lie about it?

Ten

WALKING INTO SCHOOL next to Bruno is like an out of body experience. From the second we hit the first step, people are waving and saying hello, not just to Bruno who is literally friends with everyone in the school, but to me as well. I'm getting looks of abject shock mixed with lust from most of the male population, and the girls are either shooting daggers with their eyes or sighing wistfully. I'm not sure which of these things makes me feel more like I'm walking naked into a gauntlet.

My first class of the day is with Coach Mason. He's wearing his usual white shirt, buttoned almost to his neck with the sleeves rolled up around his elbows, and Dockers. I walk in just a heartbeat before the bell. He's writing on the chalk board and when he turns and sees me, he's momentarily confused.

"Hey Mr. Mason." I say and scope out a seat. The front two rows are completely filled with females, including Kaylee herself. I make my way to a back seat and an empty desk next to Carson who greets me warmly.

As Bruno predicted, there was no announcement about Logan's death, no plans for a memorial at the school, and no grief counselors. The day went like any other day, except for the part where people were actively talking to me. Okay, mostly guys, but even a few girls strike up convos with me throughout the day. It's like going from being invisible to being a celebrity. I try to be kind, and mostly to refrain from insulting anyone, even when they say things like *irreguardless* and speak in annoying text acronyms, *and I was like, OMG, NW. IDBY.*

However , by the end of third period, I am actually trembling with the need to slap the girl in my journalism class who keeps telling me how *super much* she wanted to *learn journalism* so she can get into Fashion Week free and sit up front.

By the time the bell rings and I gather my books, Bruno and his friends Becker and Cassidy are waiting for me outside the classroom door. Becker is tall and spindly, his red hair combed so it falls over his eye. He has his arm around Cassidy, a busty short blonde girl with a smattering of freckles across her nose. The ultimate odd couple.

"Hey," Bruno says, taking my books.

I let myself grab him with one arm and hug him gently. Logan is standing beside him, and I don't think I've ever been so glad to see anyone in my life. It's so weird how I've gotten so used to having him around in such a short period of time.

"How was class?" Cassidy asks me cheerfully.

"Well, I didn't strangle anyone, so I count that as a raging success."

She smiles warmly. "You guys getting ready to start yearbook orders?"

I nod. "Yeah, actually we are opening up for orders next week. Just working on layout so we have an estimate of how much printing is gonna cost."

"Can't they just estimate based on the page count from last year?" Becker asks, flicking his head to get the hair out of his eyes.

I pause, "Yeah. We will do that. But they are talking about adding a few pages. I think they want to put together some kind of memorial for Logan."

It's only half a lie. The memorial was my idea. It'll give me an excuse to get pictures and talk to people about him, specifically Kaylee. A stroke of genius, if I do say so myself.

"Clever," Logan mumbles, looking reluctantly impressed.

"May I walk you to lunch?" Bruno asks, holding out his arm as I weave mine through.

"That'd be wonderful."

Becker tisks. "Quit being so chivalrous. You're making the rest of us look bad, dude."

Bruno beams as we head for the parking lot.

One of the nicest things about being a senior is off campus lunch privileges I decide, as we pile into Becker's Rubicon. Not that our tiny town has a lot of options, but tradition dictates that at least for the first day, we eat at The Melting Pot. The pizza is to die for and it has all the charm of a 1970's head shop.

The large round table in the very back is already full of Logan's friends. Everyone is there. Darla, head cheerleader and the only person on the planet under the age of fifty who actually plays the harp, Katelyn and Abygail Rodgers, aka the twins, Austin Lattimer, whose mother is the town Mayor, and of course, Jesus DePalma, who is built like a NFL linebacker and has a mowhawk, earning him the moniker Mr. T. Even Becca and Madison are there, somehow having detached themselves from Kaylee's ass for five minutes.

The only person missing is Kaylee.

"Hey guys," Bruno says, pulling out a chair for me. "You all know Zoe, right?"

They take turns murmuring hello with varying degrees of enthusiasm. Katelyn and Abygail seem genuinely pleased to meet me officially for the first time (though we've shared classes for three years) and Austin and Jesus are equally kind and friendly. The lemmings couldn't care less that I'm there and Darla looks legitimately put out. Then I remember that she and Bruno dated for a few months last year. No wonder she's giving me scorpion eyes.

The waitress comes over and the guys proceed to order.

"Two large pepperoni with extra cheese and light sauce please," Jesus says.

"And I need a salad," Darla chimes in, with a few of the other girls asking for the same.

"And I need a medium deep dish with pepperoni, jalapeño, pineapple, and bacon," I add.

The twins stare at me in abject horror. I look over at Bruno, sure I've committed some cardinal sin, but he's just grinning. The waitress brings over a massive pitcher of soda and the conversation begins.

Logan has sprawled out in the booth next to us and he's watching the group intently.

"Where's Kaylee?" he asks suspiciously.

I look around the table. "Where's Kaylee?"

Madison makes a show of flipping her blonde hair. "She said she had other plans. Can you believe that?"

The guys could really care less, but thankfully Darla is intrigued enough to ask a follow up. "Plans? Plans with who?"

"With *whom*," Logan corrects from his booth making me want to give him a big grammar Nazi high five.

Madison shrugs, but Becca leans over and whispers conspiratorially. "I think it's the new mystery guy she's seeing."

Darla clanks the ice in her cup with the straw. "Who cares?" she says bitterly.

Madison and Becca are on the Dance Committee so I decide to change the subject.

"Hey, just so you know, we picked a date and a theme for Homecoming," I say, feigning enthusiasm.

"Well, it was actually Leena's idea. We are doing Venetian Masquerade."

Becca swoons. "Ooo. I love that." She turns to Madison and they immediately start planning. "We could do one of those little boats for people to take their picture in."

"A gondola," I say helpfully.

"Right. And we can drape a bunch of blue and black sheer fabric from the ceiling and put little white lights underneath so it looks like the night sky," Madison taps her chin thoughtfully.

"And everyone can wear beautiful masks," Darla says, visibly warming to the idea. Then her tone sours. "Maybe Kaylee will show up with her new guy, you know, since we won't be able to see his face."

"What's that supposed to mean?" Madison asks meekly, like she's unsure if something just flew over her head.

Darla smirks. "Well obviously he's completely ugly and deformed if she's ashamed to be seen with him. She probably pulled an Anna Nicole and she's dating some rich old guy on life support."

Becca makes a disgusted face and Madison laughs. Aby almost shoots soda out her nose.

"Well, whoever he is, I feel for the guy," Austin says and the other guys nod in agreement.

"Why do you say that?" I ask.

"Let's just say that a vicious, man eating piranha would probably make a better girlfriend."

Bruno waves the waitress over for another pitcher. "Yeah. Logan deserves a friggin medal for putting up with her for so long."

"Deserved," Darla corrects, sending a ripple of tension through the group.

They all fall silent, the tension heavy in the air.

"So, do you have a date yet?" Cassidy asks me, breaking the silence.

I can actually feel the relief rush in like a cool breeze. "Yeah, actually. Bruno asked me."

Across the table Austin leans forward, giving Bruno a very manly fist bump.

Jesus whistles. "Nicely done dude."

Becker just rolls his eyes and mumbles. "About time, too."

The pizzas arrive and the group breaks into discussions of lacrosse, hateful teachers, and summer vacation recaps. I just listen, trying to add a passively interested comment here and there. Logan finally stands up and moves behind me.

"Hey, I'm going to go look for Kaylee."

I nod, looking if as in response to something Becker is saying and Logan vanishes. He's still gone when we finish and head back to school.

No sooner am I back in school and back in class than Logan finally reappears. I shake my head just a fraction. I told him not to bug me in class.

"I know, but its Kaylee. She's in the bathroom crying. As soon as I realized where she was, I went outside and waited for her to come out. But she still hasn't. And I think…she was throwing up."

My hand launches into the air.

"Yes?" Mrs. Green, my AP European teacher, asks from behind her fifties style cat-eye glasses.

"May I have a restroom pass please?"

Eleven

I PAUSE OUTSIDE THE DOOR. Beside me, Logan looks worried. I can just faintly hear someone inside making a dry heave sound. Steeling myself, I push open the door and walk in. At the sound of my footsteps Kaylee muffles her cries and I hear her get to her feet and flush. I turn on the water like I'm washing my hands. She walks out and her normally porcelain complexion is a sickly white with a twinge of green. Her eyes are bloodshot and puffy.

"Are you alright?" I ask softly. She glares at me, as if I've just asked her for a kidney.

"Fine." She says finally, turning on the water and scooping a handful into her mouth. She swishes it around and spits it out.

"Do you need me to like, get the nurse or something?"

She looks over at me again. "I know you. From the funeral."

"I'm Zoe."

She nods, dipping her face low over the sink and rinsing out her mouth again. She clutches the sink with both hands, just taking deep breaths.

"Um, if you aren't feeling well, I can drive you home," I offer, earning me another dirty look. "Or find someone who can?"

She shakes her head.

"Why are you being nice to me?"

I tilt my head. "Because you're sick. And because, Logan and I used to be friends."

That makes her expression soften just a little. She laughs dryly.

"Logan was friends with everyone."

I nod. "Yeah he was."

She stands upright, adjusting herself in the mirror.

"Um," I point to her head. "You have a little puke in your hair."

She makes a face and turns her head, spotting the gooey strands. The sight of it makes her turn and run back into the stall yakking, head down into the toilet.

The sound and stench of it is enough to set off my own gag reflex but I manage to hold it down. I grab a handful of paper towels and wet them in the sink. Folding them into a long rectangle I step up behind her, carefully lift her hair and place it on the back of her neck.

"Thanks," she mutters, resting her head on the side of the toilet.

I press my back against the outside of the stall and slide down to a sitting position.

After a few minutes of silence she finally speaks again.

"We broke up, you know. I dumped him just before..." her voice trails off.

"I know. He uh, called me after. He was upset. And worried about you. Even after, he still cared about you, you know?"

She sits up, her eyes glassy. "He told you about the break up?"

I nod. "Yeah, he did."

"What else did he say?"

I let my head loll to the side. "Not much. Just that he was, you know, dealing with it."

She nods. "Can you hand me my purse?" She points to where it sits on the floor beside the sink.

I reach forward and grab the handle, but the snaps aren't closed and it spills all over the floor.

"Crap. Sorry," I mutter, crawling forward to clean up the mess.

"No," she yells.

But it's too late. I've already seen it. The slim white plastic stick with a pink plus sign in the little window.

I turn back to her, "Kaylee, are you?"

She snatches up her bag, stuffing everything back inside. Tears are running down her face, taking her mascara with it.

"Don't. You can't say anything to anybody. I mean it. If I find out you told anybody—"

I jump to the defensive. "You'll what? Beat me

with the diaper bag?"

As soon as the words are out I regret them.

"Hey, I'm sorry. I won't say anything. I promise." Reaching out I touch her arm gently. "Did Logan know?"

She shakes her head.

"I only found out last week."

"What are you going to do? I mean, that's none of my business. Is there anything I can do?"

She gets to her feet, wiping her eyes.

"Yeah. You can keep your dammed mouth shut and leave me alone." She pushes past me and storms out of the bathroom. I walk out the door and she's already down the hall, almost to the front doors.

Logan is sitting on the floor, his back pressed against the lockers.

I look down the hall to make sure we're alone.

"So, I assume you heard that."

He nods.

"You okay?"

He shakes his head no. I take a deep breath. After a few seconds he looks up.

"It's not mine, Zoe. It can't be."

I scratch my head.

"So, I don't know what you've heard, but it can happen. Even when, you know, you're careful. Condoms aren't made of lead."

He stands up, staring at me intently.

"No, you don't understand. It can't be mine. We haven't been together in like six months."

That surprises me.

"Really?" I pause, letting the info sink in. "Six months?"

"Zoe, I swear. Whatever's going on, that's not my kid."

I frown.

"I believe you. It's just…"

"Shocking?" he offers.

Then I think about Kaylee. Shocking really isn't the right word.

"Sad."

I head back to class just before the bell rings. I have every intention of keeping her secret. No reason to tell anyone, in a town this size, everyone will know soon enough. If there's one thing worse than being invisible, it's being the town slut, and that's exactly what's about to happen to Kaylee. Mega bitch or not, no one deserves that.

The day rolls on and Bruno drives me home. As we pull into my driveway he puts the truck in park and turns to face me.

"So listen, Zoe. I was wondering if, I mean I know we haven't been hanging out that long," he pauses, rubbing the back of his neck. "I mean, I guess what I'm asking is, will you, do you want to be, my girlfriend?"

From the back seat Logan grumbles.

"Kiss the poor guy before he has a stroke."

Leaning forward slowly I stretch up, pressing my lips to his. Bruno reaches up and touches the side of my face, cupping my cheek.

My stomach lurches. Not because of the kiss, but because I feel like I'm the worst person on the planet. I open my eyes, pulling away, but Bruno isn't finished with me yet. He grins and leans in for another kiss.

I feel Logan vanish even though I don't see it. As soon as he's gone I feel the pressure in the cab of the truck relax and I allow myself to be drawn into Bruno's arms. He's strong and warm and he smells like summer grass. I feel a deep ache grow in the pit of my stomach. My skin flushes and my heartbeat quickens. I feel him smile against my lips.

He draws away, catching his breath.

"I take that as a yes."

I nod. "Yes."

Logan is waiting for me in my room. He's pacing, looking like he's about to scream. I can't blame him. Finding out his ex girlfriend is knocked up by some other dude has to suck royally.

"You alright?" I ask, tossing my messenger bag on the bed and flopping down to take off my shoes.

He makes a face. "Oh yeah. I'm great. My life is falling apart and you are out sucking face with my best friend."

"You told me to kiss him, you ass hat."

I throw my shoe at him and it nails him in the back.

"Forgot you were dead again, huh?" I ask with a snicker.

He glares. "How could I? I spent all day sitting in the hallway at school watching people I used to care about walk right through me."

I snort. "Welcome to my life."

He frowns and looks at me like maybe he's seeing me for the first time. And I realize he is. He's seeing life through my eyes. Our positions have been completely reversed and he hates it. My stomach churns. He hates me.

"Do you hate me?" I ask softly. "For still being alive? For being where you used to be?"

He sighs slowly. "Maybe a little." Then he turns his back to me, looking out the window. "Maybe I just hate myself for putting you there."

His expression changes and he leans forward, pressing his hands against the glass.

"What is it?" I ask, moving to his side.

He jerks his chin. "There. Across the street by the mailbox. Do you see him?"

He steps back and I take his place. I see the mailbox, Mrs. Kelly's yard gnomes guarding her front door. And a couple of kids riding by on bikes.

"No. I don't see anyone." I turn and look at Logan whose face has set in a scowl. "Is it him? The one who's been following you?"

He nods and a shiver ripples across my skin. I wrap my arms around my torso, hugging myself. Behind me, Logan steps forward. I feel him touch my arm for just a heartbeat before he goes intangible again.

"It's okay Zoe. I'm not going to let him hurt you."

I swallow hard. It's not me that I'm worried about.

Twelve

THE NEXT MORNING, Bruno shoots me a text to say good morning and asks me to meet him in the parking lot before class. He has practice after school so we're taking separate cars today. I have to admit, after our kiss last night I was almost glad he wasn't picking me up. I mean, how am I supposed to greet him now? Will he be one of those guys who likes to make out in public all the time? I'm so nervous I feel like I've swallowed a wasp's nest.

Logan watched over me all night as I tossed and turned restlessly. Nothing like good old fashioned terror to keep you up all night. Every once in a while I caught him looking at me with this soft expression. Something about it made me feel warm and safe. He'd left the room while I changed without my having to ask, then re-emerged right away. True to his word he's sticking close today, though he hasn't been his normal, chatty self. He's been stoic, a man with a lot on his mind. As I drive to school, the silence is physically painful, weighing down on me like a sack of bricks.

"So, what's the plan today?" I ask, opening up what I hope will be a safe line of communication.

He grumbles. "You know. I'm just going to hang out and be dead. Talk to myself, watch people doing things I don't get to do anymore. Smell food I can't eat. If I get really frisky I might go watch my mom cry some more."

I slam on the breaks, swerving the car onto the shoulder of the road.

"Pity party, table of one. What the fuck, Logan?"

His moods are giving me whiplash. I know he's dead and all, but seriously.

"Excuse me for having a moment of depression about the fact that I'm dead."

I turn, slinging my arm over the seatback.

"Logan, I think you are missing the obvious here. Yeah you're dead, and yeah that pretty much sucks 24-7. But you are also like, free. I mean, you said you wanted to go to New York, right? So go now. Go today. You don't even need a plane ticket. You can just blink and be there. You can go anywhere. Do anything. Sky's the limit. And let's be honest, I'm not even sure that's technically true."

He shakes his head. "Yeah. I can do anything. Except the one thing I want to do."

I take a shallow breath, too afraid to ask what he's talking about. The expression on his face is raw and full of pain. He wants to be alive. And I can't give him that. I can't even give him a half way decent death.

"Look, I will go over to Kaylee's after school and get some answers. I know how hard it is for you to be stuck here like this, with me of all people. We will get to the bottom of what happened. I promise."

He looks at me, shaking his head like I just don't understand. Maybe I don't. How could I? I have my whole life ahead of me.

Swerving back into traffic, I head for the school. As he promised, Bruno is waiting for me, standing next to his truck chatting with Becker and Austin.

"What are you going to do when I'm gone?" Logan asks suddenly as I reach in the back to grab my bag.

"What do you mean? I ask quietly, digging around a little so Bruno can't see me.

Logan jerks his head toward the truck beside us. "With Bruno. You gonna keep seeing him? Keep your place in the herd?"

His tone is cold, edged with curiosity.

I open my door, stepping out.

"I honestly don't know."

Bruno, thankfully, isn't a big PDA guy, so he settles for taking my hand, giving me a quick kiss on the cheek, and walking me into the building. As soon as my suede boots hit the tile I'm flanked by the twins, Madison joining them.

"Hey Zoe. I love your outfit," Madison gushes.

I can feel myself blushing. "Thanks. You look great too." I offer sincerely. She's wearing a tiny white skirt and deep blue blouse. Between the heels on the stilts she's wearing and the miniscule skirt, she looks like a model, all long legs and bouncy hair.

"Is that jacket Marchesa?" Katelyn asks, touching the lapel.

I look down. My dress is a flowing crème color with small flowers that hits me just above the knees, the jacket is a soft green that's got brass buttons and little cuffs. You wouldn't think you could mix a girly dress and a military style jacket, but somehow, Carlos assured me, it works.

"Yeah. Spring collection, I think." I say absently.

"Oh, we have got to go shopping together some time!" Madison begs.

"Have you picked up your dress for Homecoming yet?" Cassidy asks, joining the group.

"No, not yet."

Madison claps gleefully. "We should go this weekend. I know this amazing boutique—"

"Has anyone seen Kaylee today?" Becca cuts in, stepping into the slow moving group.

The twins shrug, Bruno mutters a, "No," before turning back to the discussion he's having with his guys. Madison shakes her head.

I frown. "I um, I saw her yesterday. She was pretty sick. I think she went home early."

Becca looks concerned, but Madison waves it off. "She's still playing the grief card to get out of class. Tacky if you ask me."

"Still," I offer as politely as I can, "Maybe you

should go check on her, Becca? I'm sure she'd appreciate it."

Becca stares at me for a second, then her gaze shifts to Madison whose face is scrunched up like she's trying to speak telepathically. Finally Becca shakes her head. "I'm sure she's fine. She'll get here when she gets here. Where were we? Planning a shopping trip?"

We reach my locker and the whole group stops, everyone talking and making jokes. It takes me a full minute to see it, to process the whole scene, but when I do, I glance over to Logan who is pressed against the wall opposite me.

"Congratulations, Zoe. You did it." He waves at the girls, who are alternately talking to me and flirting with the guys. The bell rings and no one moves, everyone looks at me expectantly. I smile. "See you guys after class."

You'd have thought I was the queen giving my subjects leave to depart my presence. Bruno kisses me quickly on the cheek and walks off with Austin, Cassidy and Becker saying a very graphic goodbye before splitting up and heading for class. The twins smile and Madison informs me that she wants to ride to lunch with me, if that's alright. I nod sweetly, trying not to look as stunned as I feel. As they bounce away I overhear Madison talking to Becca.

"…so much nicer than Kaylee. Cooler too."

As I walk past, Logan claps. "Not only have you made it into the herd, I think they just elected you their leader."

"Great," I mutter under my breath. "Queen of the lemmings."

Other than a few strangers casually striking up conversations with me as if now, for some reason, I'm worth talking to and a couple of between class PDAs with my cute new boyfriend, the day is fairly uneventful. The people gawking at me are still unnerving, but I'm getting used to it. I'd ventured over to invite Carlos, but he had already promised to help the Bio teacher get set up for a lab over lunch. He kisses me on the forehead with a promise of pizza later. He's just as surprised by my new status as everyone else and I can tell there are a million questions he's dying to ask.

"Okay, Zoe Bowie. I'll come over tonight and we can chat." He promises, hugging me tightly.

He releases me quickly and I turn to see Bruno approaching. For the tiniest moment I'm sure there is about to be some kind of macho pissing contest but Bruno just holds out his hand to Carlos, who shakes it firmly.

"Hey, I don't think we've ever met officially. I'm Bruno."

"Nice to meet you, I'm Carlos."

Bruno grins, slipping an arm around my waist.

"Zoe talks about you all the time. You wanna go with us for lunch?"

Carlos smiles widely. I guess an invitation from me isn't nearly as big a deal as an invite from Bruno. "I'd love to but I have some stuff to do here."

Bruno nods, "Tomorrow then."

"Sure, I'd like that."

And just like that Carlos is in the herd whether he wants to be or not. The grin on his face tells me he's pretty happy about it. I wave and let Bruno lead me to his truck. Glancing back over my shoulder I see Carlos give me a *What just happened?* look.

Even lunch, I have to admit, is kind of fun. I'm getting to know the twins, who are both planning on going pre-med after a gap year in Europe, and somehow, cementing my place as alpha female of the pack. At one point Madison makes a rude comment.

"I bet she ditched just to meet up with her new mystery guy. She's such a slut."

I lower my chin, my voice tight and strong. "Ease off. Kaylee's been going through a lot."

She laughs sourly, "How do you know what she's been going through?"

The other girls stare at me. There is challenge in her voice. I flick my hand.

"Well her boyfriend just died, she's been sick, and her best friend is calling her a slut behind her back. And those are just the headlines."

Her face puckers like I've slapped her.

"Besides, have any of you bothered to check on her? See how she's doing?"

Shamed silence. I shrug.

Becca quickly changes the subject but Madison shoots me a meek glance that is filled to the brim with guilt. Good. I may not like Kaylee, but no one deserves to be turned on by their friends.

I turn to Bruno, wrapping my arm through his. He grins and kisses me.

Cassidy sighs wistfully.

"You guys are a shoe in for Homecoming King and Queen."

I jerk my face toward her.

"Huh?" We've been dating for like three seconds and suddenly we are the plastic cake toppers?

She rolls her eyes. "Come on, everybody sees it. You two are, like the new perfect couple."

I raise an eyebrow.

Bruno leans over, whispering, "It's one of her theories on human social behavior. Cassidy wants to be a Shrink."

"Psychologist," she corrects.

"Well, you have the first part down," Darla jokes from Austin's lap. "You're already a Psycho."

Cassidy wads up a napkin and throws it at her good-naturedly, then she turns back to me.

"It's a fact that in adolescent groups, people will seek out a 'perfect couple' to emulate. They look to them for social cues on how a relationship should function."

I wrinkle my nose. "That's nice to say, I think. But no relationship is ever perfect. I mean," I look at Bruno. He's kind of perfect. Handsome, sweet, kind, and smart. He's everything a girl could want, the whole package. So why do I feel like something is missing? "We haven't even been together a full week. Eventually he's going to witness my unbelievable troll-like bed head and decide I'm not worth the trouble." I try to keep my tone light and he chuckles.

"No amount of bed head could do that," he says, kissing the tip of my nose. "Now if you were to tell me you're a Redskins fan, that might be a deal breaker."

I scrunch my face. "Redskins? Oh, you mean that practice team the Cowboys like to beat up on so much?"

That remark earns me an enthusiastic hug and a high five from Becker.

"See? She is perfect."

Katelyn is staring at me blank faced. Aby pats her hand, "Football, sweetie."

She makes an, oh face and smiles gently, blushing.

Darla digs a tall blue bottle out of her oversize purse and sets it on the table.

"What's that?" I ask.

She passes it to me, "It's Genius Water. Full of brain boosting vitamins and stuff."

I look at the label, then glance up.

"Really? You paid $5 for Genius Water?"

"Yeah why?"

"Sorry to break it to you but I don't think it's

working."

She frowns. "Of course it's expensive. It's from Paris."

"Really? Because according to the fine print it's bottled in Newark."

Beside me Bruno erupts in a fit of laughter as Darla snatches the bottle back from me.

Logan spends the whole hour sitting in an empty booth close by, staring out the window. He doesn't even glance at me once. I try not to let it bother me, but something about his posture, the fierceness in his expression has the little hairs on the back of my neck standing up. I'm sure his mystery stalker is out there, watching. Waiting.

But for what?

The rest of school is a blur. I kiss Bruno goodbye and he heads off for lacrosse practice. I know he wants me to stick around and watch, but I want to get somewhere private so I can talk to Logan.

I don't see him anywhere after school, and he's not at my car. I swallow, hoping he's not off chasing shadows. It's a long, quiet drive home and I keep hearing what Cassidy said echoing like an accusation in my ears.

The perfect couple.

Maybe we could be. Maybe we could be that blissfully happy couple everyone else looks up to. Lord knows Bruno would be an easy guy to fall for. But all I can think about right now is Kaylee and how to get her to open up to me. I can't even think of my life beyond today. I have to figure out what happened to Logan. He deserves to be at rest, at peace. Every day he spends here is like hell for him. Still a little, desperate, insane part of me doesn't want him to go. Because as long as he's here…

I don't even know how to finish that thought.

I turn the corner onto my block and see a long white unmarked police car parked in my driveway. I pull up to the curb. Logan is standing on the porch next to my mother and the two plain clothed detectives talking to her. She points in my direction.

I get out of the car and walk over to them.

Normally, I'd be panicked, but I'm calm as something is setting off alarms in my head. My fight or flight instinct must be broken, because every time those alarms go off inside me, I go straight to fight. Fleeing isn't even an option.

"Mom? What's going on?"

She pulls me close and puts her arms around me.

"It's your friend, Kaylee. Sweetie she's dead."

I pat her back, confusion fading into shock. Pulling back I look at the cops.

"What? How?"

The short black woman and her thick burly male partner exchange looks.

"We'd like you to come down to the station and answer some questions."

"Me? Why?"

Another exchange of looks.

"You don't have to go, baby," mom offers

protectively.

I shake my head. "No, Mom. It's fine."

She folds her arms, "Fine, but I'm coming too. And I'm calling our lawyer."

"You can ride with us," the man says, grabbing my arm.

I pull it away. "I'll ride with my mom. You can follow us in your car if you'd like. But first I'm going to put my backpack in my room and pee, if that's okay with you?"

The woman nods, following us into the house. She watches from the hallway as I drop my bag and enter the bathroom, closing the door.

"Logan!" I whisper as loud as I dare.

He appears beside me. I move to throw my arms around him, and he's solid. Just for a few seconds. But it's getting longer and longer each time. I can't help but wonder, if he stays long enough, maybe he could be real again? I shake away the thought.

You can't be alive without a body, my brain reminds me.

"What's going on?" I demand.

He shakes his head. "All I know is that police found her body this morning. Her parents called the police when she didn't come home last night."

"Where did they find her? What else do you know?"

He shakes his head, "Okay, don't take this the wrong way, but I'm not going to tell you. That way when the police tell you, you'll be genuinely surprised."

I frown. "Why do I need to be surprised?"

"I don't know, but I know that they think..." he lowers his face, brings us nose to nose. "They think you were involved or that you know something. This is really important, Zoe. You have to be completely honest, or at least as honest as you can be."

I nod. "This just sucks. My only alibi is a dead guy no one else can see."

He smirks. "Sorry."

I flush the toilet and turn on the sink.

"Zoe, I'll be there every second, ok? Just try to relax."

I frown. Sure relax.

Says the dead guy.

Thirteen

THE INSIDE OF THE POLICE STATION is nothing like what you see on TV. It actually looks like the freaking DMV, only a little more cheerful. The detectives lead mom and I into a big conference room looking area with a full glass wall and no windows. It's generic and sterile and reeks of burnt coffee and old spice. I take a seat at one side of the table. Starsky and Hutch stare at me across the table. I eyeball them coldly, trying to decide which one is going to play bad cop.

"Miss Reed. As your mother told you, Kaylee Greely was found dead early this morning. How well did you know Miss Greely?"

Logan stands behind the detectives, watching me. "Just be honest," he encourages.

"Not well. I knew of her. We'd spoken a few times."

"So you weren't close?"

"No, why?" I ask, irritation growing in chest like a thorny vine.

"Just answer the questions please."

"Um, I am."

Mom reaches over and pats my shoulder.

"Did you see her yesterday?"

I take a deep breath. "Yeah. At school. She was in the bathroom, crying."

I pucker, trying to decide whether to leave it there or press forward. Logan nods for me to continue.

"She was sick. Throwing up. I gave her a cool towel. And, uh, she asked me to hand her purse to her. It spilled and there was a pregnancy test inside."

They exchange another mysterious look and scribble on a big yellow pad of paper.

"I asked her about it, and she admitted she was pregnant."

"Is that all?"

I shrug. "I felt bad for her, offered to drive her home, she told me no and left on her own."

"Is that the last time you saw her."

I nod.

The chunky guy opens a file on the counter.

"Have you ever been to the Apple Mountain Radio Tower?"

I nod again.

"How long ago was that?"

"I went a few months ago with a cleanup crew, and then again about a week ago."

"For what purpose did you go all the way up there, Miss Reed?"

I clench my jaw.

"I went because…I wanted to try to understand what happened to Logan."

"Were you and Logan close?"

I nod. "Best friends when we were little. And we had recently re-connected."

"What did you do at the tower?"

I stop, glaring at them both. "What are you accusing me of?"

"They think you might have had something to do with it, just be honest, Zoe. Tell them everything. If you lie about anything, it will only make it worse."

"We just need you to answer the question, please."

I shrug. "I walked around. Climbed up the tower. I was just looking for…I dunno, anything that might give me some clue to who did this."

"Did what?" The short woman asks.

I pause again. Leaning forward I put my palms flat on the table.

"For whoever murdered Logan."

I swear I see a slight twitch in her eye.

"Logan Cooper's death has been ruled a suicide."

I sit back, folding my arms across my chest.

"Nope. No way. I could almost swallow an accident, but Logan would never kill himself."

"Why do you say that?" the man asks.

I cock my head, looking directly at Logan as I speak.

"Because Logan was a pompous, arrogant, ego driven ass-hammer. He was also completely terrified of heights. No way in hell would he go anywhere near that bridge voluntarily."

"I thought you said you were friends."

"We were. Doesn't mean he was a prince. It means he was a jerk and I liked him anyway."

"Did you know that the day before he died, Kaylee ended their relationship? She said he was distraught."

I snort. "I did know that, actually. He told me. He also told me she was cheating on him, did she mention that little nugget? Or how about the fact that they hadn't had sex in months? Whoever's baby she was carrying, it wasn't his."

The guy tilts his head curiously. "Did that make you angry with Kaylee?"

"Angry? No. Why should it? I just felt sorry for her. A kid at seventeen?" I make a face. "That sucks."

"Were you having a physical relationship with Logan Cooper?"

I actually laugh out loud. "Ha, no. No."

"Is there anything else you would like to tell us Miss Reed? Anything you think of that might be helpful?"

"No." I pause, "Actually, maybe. When I was up at the tower, I found something. A silver necklace that Logan had given Kaylee. It was all broken."

"What did you do with it?"

"It's at home, in my dresser. I can bring it to you if you think it'll help. I was going to…get it fixed and give it back to her."

"Why would you do that for someone who,

according to you, you barely knew?"

I smile softly, "I figured, it was what Logan would want. He'd want her to have it."

"Do you mind if I ask what happened to your hand?" the lady points at me with the tip of her pen.

I look down. I'd completely forgotten about that. I rub it with the pad of my thumb.

"Yeah, I cut it last week, up at The Tower, actually. The bottom rung has a sharp piece of metal sticking out. I didn't see it."

"I remember that," mom chimes in. "I'm a nurse. I saw it when I got home for my shift. I helped her clean it out and get it bandaged up."

The detective closes the folder, glancing at his partner.

"We appreciate your cooperation. And we would like to come get that necklace, if you don't mind."

I nod. They stand up to leave.

"Wait, can you tell me, what happened? I mean she was sick, but she was fine."

The lady shakes her head, choosing her next words very carefully. "I'm sorry, but we can't discuss an ongoing homicide investigation."

I feel the air combust in my lungs, pain exploding in my chest.

"I'll stay here and see what I can overhear from these two. Meet you at your house later," Logan says.

I nod a silent thank you. Mom takes my hand and I let her. I realize I haven't held her hand once since dad died. As soon as we are in the fresh air I jerk her hand, pulling her into a long hug.

I don't say anything on the way home, just stare out the window. I keep thinking of Kaylee, expecting to see her pop up in my back seat. Wondering what happened.

Homicide.

Murder.

The words drill into my brain like corkscrews. First Logan, now Kaylee. Is it wrong to assume they are related? Is it even possible that they aren't? And if Kaylee was murdered, is her spirit hanging around her like Logan's is? Is she a ghost stalking some random person too? Maybe Logan and Kaylee can skip off into the afterlife together. They always were the perfect couple.

Then Cassidy's words come back to me.

Perfect couple.

Bruno and I are the new Logan and Kaylee.

Then something else clicks into place.

If Bruno and I are the new Logan and Kaylee, does that make us next on the hit list?

By the time Carlos shows up with pizza, I've thoroughly freaked myself out. There's no sign of Logan and I just feel like ants are crawling up my skin. I hear mom report the bad news to him in the hallway before he makes his way back to my room. Setting the pizza on my desk, he comes over to where I'm curled in my chair like a mental patient.

He doesn't ask if I'm okay, he just kneels down

and sets his head in my lap. I stroke his short, dark hair. Not to be outdone, Brim jumps in my lap, curling herself around his head. Carlos laughs, sits up, and sneezes.

"Why cat? Why do you hate me?"

"Aww, she doesn't hate you," I say, nuzzling my kitty. "She loves you."

He sneezes. "Yeah, loves me to death. That cat is trying to kill me."

I pet her and she curls up in my lap, purring contentedly.

"The police questioned me," I offer with a frown.

Carlos closes my door, bringing the pizza box over and folding himself into my old red bean bag. He hands me a slice, which I take, plucking a pepperoni off for Brim.

"Why?"

I shrug. "Because I'm probably the last person who saw her alive." I pause, "If you don't count the person who killed her."

"Wow. Just wow."

I take a bite and the cheese is still hot enough to burn the roof of my mouth just a little.

"I know," I mumble around the bite. "And, she was pregnant."

"Shut up!"

"It's true."

"It's like a made for TV movie. Do they have any suspects?"

I sigh, "Just me as far as I know."

He looks appalled. "They don't really think you did anything?"

I shake my head. "They have their heads so far up their own asses, I'd be surprised if they knew day from night."

"Who do you think did it? The baby daddy?"

It's not a bad theory, actually. I like it a lot better than the killer wanted to eliminate the perfect couple theory that I'd come up with.

"Maybe. Or maybe baby daddy is just some idiot frat boy who doesn't even know about the pregnancy."

"You sure it wasn't Logan's baby?"

I nod, taking another bite.

"Okay, who else wanted her dead?"

I stare at him for a minute. That could be a really long list actually. I can think of a dozen girls she bullied, and almost as many guys she managed to insult over the years.

Logan however, was a pretty likeable guy, all things considered.

"It's not just her. I think whoever killed her is the same person who killed Logan."

Now Carlos frowns, "I thought it was an accident?"

I shake my head.

"Oh double wow. Now it's really a made for TV movie."

"I'm thinking cable."

"Speaking of PG-13, what is up with you and Kyle Bruno? When did I fall asleep and wake up to find you had taken over the kingdom? What the hell Zoe?"

I shrug. "I ran into him at school last week. He asked me out after a lacrosse practice. Then we talked on the phone a few times. He offered to pick me up for school. Next thing I know, he's asking me to be his girlfriend and go to Homecoming with him."

His hands actually flutter to his mouth. For a gay guy, Carlos isn't what I'd call flaming. But every once in a while he makes an expression like this and I can't contain my laughter.

"Oh my gawd. Are we going to Homecoming?"

I nod. "And I'll need my fairy godmother to help me pick out a dress." I frown, "Oh, and the lemmings want to go too, I think."

"Okay, first of all, you have got to stop calling them that. They are *your* lemmings now and you need to keep that in mind. Seriously, Zoe. And secondly, you can't call me your fairy godmother. It's *offensive.*"

I open my mouth to apologize and he chuckles. I flip him off.

"So if I can't call them lemmings, what should I call them? Minions? Ooh, I know, groupies."

"How about friends?"

I pout. "Do I have to?"

He nods. "Yep sorry. It's part of being the leader."

"What if I don't want to be the leader?"

He chuckles again, "You should have considered that before you started dating the most popular guy in school and dressing like a model."

His eyes widen. "Hold up. Is that what the wardrobe make over was all about? Landing yourself a boy?"

I grimace. "Busted."

He folds his arms. "Zoe, I can honestly say I've never been more proud of you than I am right now. Using your feminine wiles to reel in a helpless man-fish. Albeit a very hot man-fish. Seriously."

"Feel free to shut the hell up."

"I just want to relish this moment," he says with a devious grin.

"And I want to not have to kill you and bury the body. I'm willing to do many things, Carlos, digging isn't one of them."

"And you wonder why the police suspect you of being a psychotic murderer."

I pout, "Well, they never actually accused me of being psychotic."

"Only because they don't know you."

I stand up, setting Brim on the floor beside Carlos. She immediately begins rubbing herself against him. He sneezes.

"That's low, Zoe."

I shrug. "Kitten bomb. New weapon in the field of allergen warfare."

He gently brushes Brim aside. "Just remember, that with great popularity comes great responsibility."

I raise an eyebrow.

He sighs. "I mean, Kaylee used her powers for

evil. Remember that girl freshman year that ended up in the hospital because Kaylee called her fat so she stopped eating?"

"How could I forget? I always thought Kaylee should put that on her resume someday. Or the time that guy in her Chemistry class accused her of cheating so she had the football team push his Jeep into the pool?"

He nods. "Classic Kaylee. But that's what I'm talking about. What if you used your newfound popularity to actually make people's lives a little better, instead of making people's lives miserable?"

"I'm intrigued. What are you thinking?"

"Well, like, you know that the debate team just lost their funding and they can't afford to travel to state this year."

I frown. "No, I actually didn't know that."

"I heard one of the kids in my history class talking about it. Anyway, what if the student council—backed by you and your new friends—did a fundraiser or something to help them out?"

"I like it." I grab a piece of paper and a pencil and hand it to him. "Here, let's keep a list of ideas."

Wiping his hands on his slacks he starts scribbling. When he's finished, he chews absently on the eraser.

"What else?" I ask

"You could ask the principal to extend off campus lunch privileges to underclassmen. It would help with the crowding issues a little."

I hold up my hands. "Whoa, what do I look like,

a miracle worker?"

He tilts his head, "No you look like the reigning Queen of Royal Oak High School."

I shake my head. "Kaylee was the queen."

"The queen is dead. Long live the queen."

I fight off a shudder.

Carlos spends the better part of the evening coming up with causes for me to champion, everything from vending machines to bigger lockers. There's no way I could accomplish even half of the things he's scribbling down. Still, he loves making lists and he's right. I might actually be able to do some good my last year of high school. When he hands me the list I can feel my eyes welling up with tears.

"Are you crying?" He asks, his tone shocked.

I make a face. "Pfft. No. My eyeballs are sweating."

He chuckles. "Okay, this is me. What's up?"

I take a deep breath, trying to steady myself before I speak. The emotions are washing over me so quickly I feel like I'm in an estrogen blender. What is my problem?

I rub at the corner of my eye. "I suppose I just thought…I thought I'd go all the way through high school as a nobody, you know? Like, I figured no one would ever see me, ever care what I thought or what I did. Now it's like—"

"Everyone is watching."

I nod. "Exactly. I went from being invisible to being the center of attention overnight. All by not actually being myself. I feel like a total fraud."

As soon as the words are out, I feel the truth of them aching into my bones. I'm a fraud as a girlfriend, a fraud as a friend, and a fraud as a leader. I may have convinced myself I was doing it to help Logan, but deep down, I wanted to be *seen*. And now I am. And all I can think is how quickly I would give it all back if it meant Logan didn't have to be dead.

I suck in a sharp gasp.

"What Zoe?"

I look up at Carlos, waiting patiently for me to spill my guts to him. But the thing is, I can't. I can't ever say the words that are eating away at my soul. Not out loud, to him or anyone else.

I'm in love with Logan.

I cover my mouth with my hand to keep from laughing hysterically. Of course I'm in love with Logan. He's the very epitome of the unattainable hero. Handsome, smart, a giant pain in the ass sure, but he's also a really good guy. He's perfect actually, except for the fact that he's dead.

Oh sure. I have a perfectly great guy—one who is still breathing—and the popularity I always wanted. And what do I do? I go and fall for the dude with no pulse.

There is something so very, very wrong with me.

Inside my mind something flashes. What if Logan isn't really haunting me? What if I've had some sort of a mental breakdown? It would actually be more plausible than the truth.

"I wonder."

"What?" Carlos asks, grabbing another slice of pizza.

"I wonder if there's some kind of support group for people who are my brand of crazy."

Carlos winks, "Oh sugar, I doubt it."

When Carlos leaves it's after nine and I'm lying in bed, the covers pulled up to my chin, flat on my back and staring at the ceiling. I'm trying to think back, trying to isolate the point when I lost my mind. It's harder than it sounds because, let's face it, I've been a mess since the day my dad died. I play it over and over in my head, the funeral, seeing Logan in the coffin. Everything rolls through my brain over and over in Technicolor. My stomach is churning and my mouth is watering like I might actually throw up. And I'm so cold I'm shivering all over.

Shock.

I think I'm in shock.

Maybe I should call my mom?

As soon as the thought comes, Logan appears in my room. I feel him more than I see him. The lights are all off, the blinds are closed and the curtains drawn. I've even unplugged my alarm clock. It's just darkness and a hint of shadow.

"Zoe, are you alright?"

The sound of his voice unspools a ribbon of pain inside my hollow chest. I squeeze my eyes closed. Out of nowhere my overhead light flips on. I jerk upright in bed.

Logan is standing there, his hand still hovering over the switch. He glances from it to me, his face just as surprised as I'm sure mine is.

"What's wrong?" he asks, moving to the foot of my bed and sitting down. I curl my feet out of the way, flopping back down.

"I got accused of murdering your girlfriend today. Cut me some slack." My voice is bitter and cold, sharper than I mean for it to be. But everything is so raw, I feel like if I don't strike out at someone—anyone—I'll just end up cutting myself to shreds.

"Yeah, about that. I followed the cops for a while. Sounds like you were their best lead, but when you were able to explain everything...well, let's just say they believed you and that's all that matters."

"So do they have any other leads? Anything at all?"

He sits back, curling his legs under him, leaning back against the footboard.

"Not really. They are looking for the mystery guy she was seeing. But other than that, nothing. They said she was only a few weeks pregnant, so there's no chance of recovering any DNA."

"And even if they could, they would have to have a guy to match it to, which they don't."

"Exactly. So I went back to The Tower, that's where they found her body. They think she was thrown off the top."

I shiver, adding another layer of goosebumps to my skin.

"And they are sure she didn't just jump?"

"I guess she'd been pretty badly beaten up first. I saw her body. In the morgue. I just—"

His voice cracks. I fight not to look at him, I don't want to see the pain in his eyes. I have enough of my own emotional damage to deal with.

"Anyway, afterwards I went to her house, to the cemetery, the school. Anywhere I could think of."

I swallow and it feels like hot coals going down my throat. "You went looking for her. For her ghost."

"I didn't find anything. Noting except that ring wraith that's been following me. He got really close to me tonight at the cemetery, Zoe. I thought... I just had this feeling like if he touched me, I would disappear. Like he'd eat my soul. I freaked out and screamed at him. I asked him if Kaylee was gone."

I wait, not moving. I'm completely paralyzed, even my lugs aren't working.

"He didn't answer, not that I could hear, but I sort of felt it. It's hard to explain. But Kaylee isn't here. He's not a ghost."

"Do you think he got to her, this Reaper?"

He hesitates. "Reaper? As in the Grim Reaper?"

Another long pause.

"Yeah, I guess that makes sense. I mean, he even looks like the Grim Reaper. I guess I always thought it was just nonsense."

"Like ghosts?"

"Point made. But no, I don't think he did anything

to her. I think she just moved on the way she was supposed to."

I roll my eyes. "If she got into heaven, I'm going to file a formal complaint."

He chuckles. I sit up slowly, letting my bitterness cover the pain like a balm, numbing everything inside me.

"She was our best lead, Logan. What are we supposed to do now?"

He shakes his head. "When I went back to The Tower, I sort of remembered something else."

"What?"

"I remember driving up to The Tower that night. I just wanted to be alone. Only her car was in the parking lot. I parked, opened my door, and that's when I heard it."

"What?"

"A struggle. I heard her screaming. I started the engine back up and drove through the trees into the clearing beside The Tower. I remember seeing her in my headlights. She was..."

"What damn it?"

"Naked. She was naked."

"Holy shit dude."

"I remember thinking, what is going on? Like, I thought she was running from someone. But it wasn't fear on her face, it was surprise. She wasn't alone. She was..."

I hold up my hand. "Ok, no details please. I'd like very much not to throw up tonight, thank you."

"You get the idea."

"Wait, so you saw the guy? The mystery guy?"

"Yeah, but the thing is, I can't remember his face."

"You think he killed you."

"Well someone did, and I doubt it was Kaylee."

"And then, he killed her too."

He nods again. His face is ashen, his cheeks hollow. His eyes are rimmed in red. I reach out, not thinking, and take his hand. He feels solid under my fingers.

I sigh when the feeling of his skin finally fades away.

"It's getting longer each time I touch you. I can feel you longer."

He half smiles, running a finger lightly over the top of my hand. I can feel it, like someone is rubbing an ice cube on my skin.

"What do you think it means?"

He sighs heavily. "I don't know. But I feel like, we have to figure out what happened to me, and soon. I don't want that Reaper anywhere near you."

I frown, "I don't think he's here for me, Logan."

"No, but if he comes for me and you get caught in the crossfire..." His voice drops to a whisper. "I don't know what I'd do if anything ever happened to you, Zoe."

My breath hitches in my throat.

"Probably have to find a new girl to stalk," I say, trying to break the tension. But he looks up, his eyes melting into mine. He scoots forward, our faces only inches apart. Reaching up he tucks a strand of hair behind my ear, tracing his fingertips along the curve of my jaw. My heart launches into an uneven gallop because I can feel him. The pads of his fingers and the warmth of his breath are real. Or maybe I just want to feel him so desperately that my mind is playing tricks. I don't know. Don't care.

I just don't want it to end.

"Zoe," he whispers my name softly, like a plea or a prayer. His voice is thick with longing and it rolls along my skin like the breaking tide.

I can't breathe, can't move. It's like the world is dying and being born all around me over and over. I should say something, *do* something, but I'm on fire, combusting from the inside out.

He presses his lips to mine and I'm undone. All thought and reason and logic are burned away in a ball of fire. I close my eyes, letting the world around us melt away. My body aches and throbs and all I can smell is Logan, cool and fresh like spring water, all I can feel is his mouth moving on mine, desperate and passionate. I run my hands up the back of his neck, weaving my fingers through his hair. He pulls me against him and the ache inside me grows, painful and raw. I'm burning like a star, I can feel the heat inside me, almost unbearable, and I don't know how long I can contain it.

A cold wind whips through the room, hitting me like a bucket of ice water. I pull back, shivering and numb, grasping at air. Logan blinks, then spins, leaping to his feet. His body goes rigid and for the first time I can see why.

I can see The Reaper.

Fourteen

I'M STILL FROZEN, ONLY NOW IT'S LITERAL, like having the worst case of frostbite in history. My fingers and toes are numb, my face bitter cold. I can actually see my breath in the air.

"What do you want from me?" Logan demands.

The hooded figure doesn't answer. It just stands there, long brown robe pooling on the floor around it, hood drawn so its face is hidden in shadow. Raising a hand it points, past Logan to me.

"You can't have her. I won't let you touch her."

Logan is defiant and bold, stepping toward the creature, his hands balled into fists at his side.

It shakes its head slowly.

Stepping forward, Logan throws a punch, but his fist passes through the figure. He rocks back, surprised.

"Just take me instead," Logan pleads softly. "Leave her alone and take me."

I lunge forward, finally able to move. I can feel the adrenaline course through my veins like acid, burning away the cold.

"No!" I reach for Logan, but he's a ghost again and I can't make contact with him. He turns to look at me.

"Logan, don't you dare give yourself up to that freak."

He shakes his head. "I don't think we have a choice."

I back up, moving to the edge of my bed. "Please, Logan. I don't want to lose you. Not yet. It's not fair."

His face falls and he turns away from me, back to The Reaper.

I back myself into the corner of my bed, reaching blindly behind me. Wrapping my fingers tightly around a metal rod I race forward, swinging at The Reaper wildly. The fireplace poker connects, dropping the creature to its knees. As I draw back for another blow it vanishes.

"That's what I thought, you pathetic Ghost-of-Christmas-Future wanna be." I drop the iron rod to the floor with a thud. Running to Logan I find that I still can't touch him.

"Sorry," I say shaking my head. "I couldn't let him take you."

He looks past me to the iron rod.

"How long have you had that in here?"

I shrug. "Since the cemetery."

"Well, good thinking. And, uh, thanks for not using that on me."

"No problem."

Neither of us says anything else, we just sort of

stand there, the discomfort growing between us. How does a passionate kiss turn into awkward silence? Like this, I suppose. I want to say something, but I can't think of anything that doesn't make me sound like a total freak so I clamp my mouth shut. It's Logan who finally breaks the silence.

"I don't want to leave you either Zoe." His eyes grow dark, "But I will do whatever I have to do to keep that thing away from you. Even if it means moving on."

I draw in a deep breath and nod once.

"Besides, you have a boyfriend. With a pulse." He tries to smile but it's lopsided and forced. "I mean, it's kind of a minimum requirement."

"Bruno is a great guy. But he's not—"

"Dead?"

I look up, trying to fight back the tidal wave of emotions threatening to overtake me.

"You. He's not you."

Logan walks over, closing the gap between us and lays a gentle kiss on my forehead. I can almost feel it, but not quite. Whatever magic allowed him to be solid for so long was gone now. And the loss of it is almost enough to make me cry.

"Get some sleep Zoe. We will figure everything out in the morning."

"What are you going to do?"

"Oh, you know. I'll just hang out in the chair over there and check out some late night infomercials."

"You mean keep watch."

He nods, "Yes. Keep watch. But something tells me that thing won't bother you again tonight, now that it knows you're armed and dangerous."

He breaks into a grin. "You are the only girl I've ever met who is ballsy enough to take on a ghost with a fireplace poker while in her rubber ducky pajamas."

I shrug.

He motions for me to crawl back in bed. But my heart is still racing and I'm sure I won't be able to sleep. I just lay there, staring at him. Maybe, I can memorize his face, every last detail. Make it perfect in my memory so that once he's gone...

The pain is sharp and crushing, like a vice around my heart.

"Logan, stay with me."

He tilts his head, "I'm not going anywhere."

I bite my bottom lip and pull back my covers. "No, stay here, with me. Beside me."

I hear the quake in my voice. "I mean, I know we can't...I just want to sleep beside you. Just once."

He grins and slips into bed beside me, so we are face to face. I draw the covers up but they fall right though him. I laugh dryly, not sure what I expected. He props his head up on his elbow.

"Now get some sleep, Zoe. I'll be here when you wake up."

"You better be."

I'm still fast asleep in Logan's arms when my mother throws open my door.

"Zoe! Get up. You missed your alarm. You're late for school."

I sit up slowly, rubbing my eyes. Mom is staring at me like I'm crazy.

"Are you sick?" she asks immediately, prepared to go into full on nurse mode on me.

I hold up a hand, trying not to smile because Logan is lying beside me snickering.

"No. No, I'm fine. Just overslept. I'll get ready. Thanks."

Mom nods warily and shuts the door. I laugh and fall back into bed.

"You know, that's the first time I've ever been busted in bed with a girl, and your mom didn't even seem to care."

I roll my eyes. "It helps that she can't actually see you."

"Good point. Maybe we should sleep like this every night."

"Fine by me," I mutter snuggling up to him.

He slides out of bed. I sigh deeply.

"We could play hooky today. Stay here, watch infomercials, lick stuff," I wag my eyebrows suggestively.

He chuckles. "Better not. I'd hate to be to blamed

for your sudden academic decline."

I wave him off. "Yes, I'm sure my poor grades are the absolute be all and end all of your afterlife."

I grab my towel and head for the bathroom and a nice long shower. When I get back to my room, Logan is on my bed, looking pensive.

"So about today's plan. I think I should go ahead and break up with Bruno. I mean, that way he'll still have time to find another date for—"

Logan cuts me off before I can finish the thought. "Why would you break up with Bruno?"

The question surprises me, I stop rummaging around in my closet to stare at Logan, whose face is stern.

"Um. Well, I thought you...and last night we... I'm confused."

He nods, licking his lips and staring at his feet.

"Zoe, you know we can't be together, right? Not really. Not in any sort of way that counts."

I almost drop my towel. Crossing the room I flop down into the chair, my knees weak.

"But, I thought we..." I shake my head. "I thought you feel the same way about me that I feel about you."

He crosses the room, kneeling at my feet and looking up at me, his eyes glassy.

"And I do Zoe. But, as you keep pointing out, I'm dead."

I shrug, "So? We can work around that."

He rolls his eyes. "It's not a lifestyle choice. I'm not short or deformed or a Ginger. I'm dead. No one can see or hear me."

"I can."

"I know. And I can't tell you how grateful I am for that, but Zoe, be realistic. We can't date. We can't go to the movies together; I can't take you to Homecoming. I can't even kiss you."

I feel the blush flood my face. "Well, sometimes you can kiss me."

He shakes his head, "And that's weird, right? I mean, what is that about? I'm not coming back to life, I don't even have a body. I'm nothing but a desiccated corpse."

I frown. "You say desiccated corpse like it's a bad thing."

"It is. It means, I'm not getting more alive, I'm just getting better are being dead."

I swallow. I'd already considered everything he's saying and disregarded it.

"I don't care. I just don't want to lose you."

"But you didn't think that through. Sure, we can hang out here, in your room, alone. And then what happens when you go off to college? Do I just haunt your dorm? And what about when you grow up, start getting older? You are going to want a life and a family and those are all things I can't give you, I can't even be part of that." He pauses, steeling his resolve. His next words are like a blade through my heart. "And it's not fair of you to ask me to watch while you sacrifice your life for some kind of half-life with me."

The tears spill over my eyes, rolling down my cheek. "Don't you dare tell me what I'm going to want. Don't you dare put this on me."

He reaches up to touch me but I push through him, walking back to the closet.

"Fine. I get it." I say with all the venom I can muster. The words going around and around in my head are the same over and over again. He doesn't love me enough to want to stay with me.

"Zoe, please. I need you to understand."

I turn back, squaring my shoulders. "I get it, Logan. I do. You need to move on. We both do. Fine."

I drop my towel. Logan spins around so quickly I'm surprised he doesn't fall over. I dress slowly, staring daggers into his back the whole time. My phone vibrates and I check it. It's a text from Bruno wondering where I am. I text him back quickly.

Got up late. Be there soon. See you after first period.

I toss the phone in my messenger bag and quickly brush out and blow dry my hair. Logan watches me intensely the entire time. As soon as I'm ready, looking killer in my tall brown boots and a short denim skirt with a white camisole and light blue sweater, if I do say so myself, I head for my car without bothering to say a word to Logan.

"Are you angry?" he asks as I back quickly out of the driveway.

I slam the stick into gear and peel out.

"You are a complete idiot, you know that Logan?"

He sighs. "Yeah, I'm getting that. But can you do me one favor today?"

I crack my knuckles. "What is that?"

He pauses before answering. "Just don't... don't kiss Bruno, okay?"

I snort. Yeah, because I'm going to let some idiotic, insecure, douche grenade tell me what to do, or for that matter, who to kiss.

"Kiss my ass, Logan. We're doing this my way now."

He sits back in his seat, folding his arms across his chest looking downright grumpy. Good. A little suffering is good for the soul.

I walk in late to first period, but Coach Mason doesn't seem to care. Next to me Carson leans over.

"Everything okay?" he whispers.

I nod. Logan, in all his dickishness has decided to take up residence inside the classroom, and he's standing next to the door, glaring at me. I'm tempted to flip him off, but instead I smile widely at Carson.

"Fine. Thanks for asking."

After class I wait for the rest of the people to file out, taking my time packing up my stuff. When they are all gone and Coach Mason has gone back into the tiny office adjoining the classroom I walk over to where Logan is still standing, still glaring.

"You might as well go home Logan," I tell him sharply. "I don't really need you here."

He huffs. "I'm going to keep watching out for you,

just like I promised. Even if you don't like it."

"Oh really? And what are you going to do if The Reaper does show up? Yell at him until he goes away?"

"Okay, I know you're pissed off at me but—"

"No buts Logan. If you want to figure out who killed you so you can move on or whatever, you'd be a helluva lot more helpful over at The Tower, trying to jog your memory than you will be here, stalking me."

"What if The Reaper comes back?"

"I've got that handled, just like I did before. So you can really go now. You know," I pause, watching as Bruno heads for my classroom door, "Unless you feel like sticking around while I make out with my boyfriend."

He makes a disgusted sound and leans over, "I do love you, Zoe. And no amount of bitchiness is going to change that." Then he vanishes.

I take a deep breath as Bruno strides into the room, grabs me around my waist, lifts me off the ground and spins me around, finally lowering me into a deep, long kiss. He's nothing like Logan really. He's muscled differently and he smells like grass and grease. And even as he's kissing me, and little butterflies are fluttering around in my stomach of their own accord, I can't help but wish he were Logan.

Heaven help me.

Fifteen

I DON'T SEE LOGAN FOR THE REST OF THE DAY, and by the time the last bell rings, it feels like a little piece of myself is missing. I'm hurt and angry and confused.

"Why don't you come hang out for practice today?" Bruno begs. His brown eyes are like a puppy dog and despite the fact that all I want to do is go home, curl up, and die, something about his offer makes me smile.

I nudge Carlos who has just come up beside me.

"What do you think, Carlos? Wanna hang out and keep me company while I watch Bruno kick some ass and take some names?"

"And ogle sweaty guys in shorts? You had me at hello, Zoe."

I chuckle and Bruno grins.

"See you out there," he says, kissing me goodbye quickly.

I hesitate just a fraction of a second, Bruno doesn't seem to notice but Carlos sure as hell does. As we walk outside to the bleachers to await the team, he grabs my arm, shaking me gently.

"Spill it Zoe, or god help me I'll beat it out of you like candy out of a piñata."

I sigh. "As per the usual, I have no idea what you are talking about."

We take a seat on the warm metal bleachers, just one row up from the bottom. Even though the day is chilly, the sun has warmed the metal, making it surprisingly pleasant on my butt.

"I know that look. It's love. You're in love."

I raise one eyebrow, "You're kidding right? I'm freaking miserable."

"Exactly. And a lot of things can make you miserable, but your level of miserable is only brought on by one thing. And that's being miserably in love."

When I don't protest he sits back, looking pleased with himself.

"So? Spill it already. Please tell me Kyle Bruno isn't as perfect as he seems. But know that if he's done anything really terrible, I will break his arms for you."

"Aww, that's the nicest thing anyone has ever said to me," I offer honestly, giving him a big bear hug.

He pats my back. "Good. Because I will. Speaking of bodily harm, I got a text from Scott. He wants to meet my parents."

I feel my eyes widen. Just because his parents are fairly relaxed about his sexual orientation doesn't mean they want him bringing his boyfriends home, or at least that is what Carlos told me once. Maybe things have changed. The semi-panicked expression on his face tells me otherwise. Carlos' mom is a retired model, and his dad used to be a pro boxer. Neither of those things makes me think that a family dinner with the new guy could go anything but sideways.

"What are you going to do?"

"I'm open to suggestions."

I think about it for a second.

"Okay, think casual. Go for dinner in, since any dead bodies will be better dealt with in private than public, and pick something your dad enjoys, so that he'll be more relaxed." I snap my fingers, "I got it. Why don't you invite him over for pizza and to watch the title fight next weekend?"

He looks at me like I'm a genius. "That's perfect. See? I knew you'd have some brilliant idea."

He pauses for a second as the team takes the field. A few other people, mostly girlfriends, take to the stands, none sitting within ear shot of us.

"Your turn. Seriously Zoe, spill it. What's going on?"

There is no possible way to explain all the weirdness so I just shake my head.

"You don't want to talk to your best friend about it, fine. That's up to you, but do me a favor, just don't torch it."

I sit back, staring at him blankly.

"Torch what?"

He jerks his head toward Bruno on the field.

"That. You get things in your head and you let them spin you around, then, instead of toughing it out, you just burn it to the ground around you. You always have."

I frown. Do I really do that?

As if seeing the question on my face, Carlos continues, "Remember last year when you got that study abroad offer? You couldn't decide if you wanted to go because you were afraid of leaving your mom alone? So what did you do? You went out to some stupid frat party, got hammered, and let yourself get busted by your mom who grounded you into infinity and told you that you couldn't go because you weren't responsible enough."

I shift in my seat. It hadn't been a deliberate choice, not something I did on purpose. It just sort of happened.

"You didn't want to deal with it, so you just tanked yourself instead of face up to it. It's a very unhealthy pattern. And Bruno, I think he might be really good for you. So don't tank it just because you are scared or confused. Give it a chance, ok?"

Where is a wall when you really need to bang your head against it?

Across the field I see Logan appear just outside the door to the school. He waves for me to go over.

"I'll be right back. I need to go get a drink from the vending machine."

"Cool. Bring me back a Diet Dew."

I nod and walk over, slamming into the door more forcefully than is really necessary.

"Still pissed I see," he says, following me down the hall toward the vending machines.

"Nope, just tired of running around in circles. Did you remember anything else?" I stuff my hand in my bag, digging around looking for some change.

"I did, actually. A car."

I roll my eyes. "Great, can you be more specific?"

"A black sedan. And there was something else, there was something hanging from the rear view mirror."

"What?"

He shakes his head. "It was dark and I didn't get a good look, but I think it was one of the team medals from last year."

I pause, change in hand. "That pretty much narrows the suspect pool down to anyone on the lacrosse team. Can you think of anyone who drives a black car?"

"I can think of two. Becker and Jesus."

"And would either of them have reason to want you dead?"

He shifts uncomfortably, his face falling into a frown. "Maybe."

"Shit, Logan. Are you really going to make me ask?"

He looks up at me. "I sort of made out with Cassidy."

What the fu—

"When?"

"The night of Bruno's pool party."

I shake my head. "You son of a—"

He holds up his hands, "Yes, I know. I'm an asshole. I was drunk and she was flirting with me and it had been so long since—"

I spin away from him, "Dude. Shut up. Seriously. I don't want to hear anymore."

"Zoe, I—"

"I mean it Logan, shut up right now or I will find the nearest piece of iron pipe and shove it up your ass. Just. Shut. Up. And let me think."

After a few minutes of intense fuming and kicking the living crap out of the soda machine resulting in two free Pepsi's I go back to Logan. I'm calm, or at least that's what I keep telling myself.

"Okay. Did Becker know?"

"I sure as hell didn't tell him."

"Well, did anyone see you?"

He shrugs. "I was really wrecked. I passed out. Don't remember much."

I swear to god, if he was alive right now, I'd kill him myself.

"Fine. Working under the assumption that he did know, do you think he'd go after Kaylee just to get back at you?"

Logan shakes his head. "Becker is a good guy. I can't think that he'd—"

"Do exactly what you did? You two-timing nut grenade."

He doesn't answer.

"Fine. At least it's something to go on. Now buzz

off while I go have a chat with Cassidy."

"You really shouldn't—"

I hold up my hand, "Seriously Logan, I'm so pissed off right now I might actually strangle you. And I might be the only person who still can. So just leave me alone. For now."

He nods and vanishes. I scoop up the sodas and head back outside.

"Hey, I asked for Diet Dew," Carlos complains.

I shrug, "Sorry, they were out. Hey, hold this for a sec, I'll be right back."

Climbing to the top of the bleachers I make my way over to Cassidy, who is sitting alone, tapping away on her phone.

I sit beside her.

"Hey, how's it going?" I ask casually.

She glances up.

"Oh, hey Zoe. What's up?"

I glance down at the field, just in time to see Bruno make a brilliant save. He glances over to see if I'm watching and I wave.

"Well, I hear that you know all the best places to go dress shopping for Homecoming. I was wondering if you wanted to go together."

She looks surprised. "I thought you were going with Becca and Madison?"

I shrug, "I like them a lot, but..." I take a deep breath. "This is my first dance. Like ever. And I'm afraid going with them might be a little overwhelming. I was hoping you and I could just go. I mean, if you want to invite them, we totally can. It's up to you."

She grins like I've totally made her day. "I'd like that. I'd like that a lot. When do you want to go?"

I pull out my phone, pretending to check my calendar even though I know I am free all week.

"I can go after school tomorrow if you have time."

"Sounds great. You wanna drive, or do you want me to?"

I nod, "Why don't you drive, and I'll buy dinner afterwards?"

"Deal."

She pushes her sunglasses off her head and down over her eyes.

"Great. Um, you can come sit with me and Carlos if you want."

She smiles again. I try to remember ever seeing her hang out with Kaylee. Every memory I have has Cassidy on the outskirts of the group, never front and center. Kind of a shame, she seems like a total sweetheart. I glance back at the field as she packs up her bag and follows me back to my seat. Becker is on the sidelines, watching us intently.

I sit down, Carlos on my right and Cassidy to my left. He pulls a pack of Twizzlers out of his bag and passes it to me. I take one and pass it to Cassidy who also takes one. Becker slides on his helmet, and I swear he's still glaring at me as he takes the field.

When practice ends I jog over to Bruno, who is

standing by the bench. Seeing me approach he drops his gear and sprints to meet me. As soon as his arms are around me he scoops me up and spins me around once, ending the embrace in a slow, deep kiss that makes my toes curl. As soon as he sets me down I feel guilt stab me in the chest like a sword.

I shake my head. "How do you do that?"

"What?" he asks curiously.

"I dunno, get so excited? Kiss me like you haven't seen me in weeks *every time?*"

He wraps his arms around my waist, locking them in the small of my back and drawing me close. "Oh, that's easy." He lowers his head, whispering in my ear, "It's because every time I get to kiss you, I feel like the luckiest guy on the planet."

Without another word I throw my arms around his neck and squeeze him against me, pressing my mouth to his. I feel myself relax against him, content to just keep kissing him for as long as he'll let me.

I sigh against his lips. So maybe it isn't the same way I feel with Logan. Maybe it's a quieter, softer emotion, but I do care about Bruno. Maybe it's selfish. Or maybe it's okay that there isn't fire and ice running through my veins every time he touches me. Maybe it doesn't have to be love. But whatever this feeling is, it's good too. And selfish or not, I just want to bask in it for a while.

He draws back for air and I reluctantly let him go. When our eyes meet, his eyelids droop drowsily, his lips are smeared with my pink shimmer, and his face is beet red. Reaching up I wipe the makeup off his face and he kisses the pad of my thumb.

Behind him Becker taps him in the back with the stick.

"Come on, loverboy. Time to hit the showers."

I nod. "You better go. See you tomorrow?"

He nods, kisses the tip of my nose, and releases me. I stand there for a second and watch him walk away. It's Carlos who comes up beside me, hugging me around the shoulders.

"Zoe, I think that boy is madly in love with you."

I widen my eyes. "God, I hope not."

"Why?"

I look up at Carlos. Enough is enough.

"I have something I need to tell you."

He takes me by the shoulders and spins me toward him.

"Zoe, are you pregnant?"

I reach out and slap him in the side of the neck.

"Ouch. A simple no would suffice." He huffs, handing me the messenger bag I forgot on the bleachers. "Then what is it?"

I swallow, not sure where or how to even begin this conversation. The last thing I want is to be hauled away to some crazy farm, but at the same time, I just need someone to talk to.

"I see dead people."

Sixteen

CARLOS PACES THE FLOOR, wearing a line into my soft brown carpet.

"Okay, I need you to go over this one more time. You see dead people?"

"Just Logan."

"Sorry, dead person."

"This is a really bad idea," Logan chimes in from my chair where he's sitting with his head in his hands.

"Shut up Logan, nobody asked you."

Carlos pauses. "And he's here right now. In this room."

I nod, "In the chair."

Carlos glances over his shoulder.

"Have you mentioned this to your mom? Maybe there's some kind of medication—"

"I'm not crazy, Carlos. Just, you know, haunted."

He shakes his head, "Right. And you can see him because?"

"Because you have secretly been harboring a torch

for me since you were five," Logan chimes in.

I flip him off.

"I don't know, okay? Because I'm a freak? Who knows? Point is, I can. And I do."

Carlos collapses to his knees, curling his legs under him and rubbing his hands through his hair and down his face.

"Okay, I'm sorry Zoe, but I need proof."

I get that. "What do you have in mind?"

He puts both hands behind his back. "How many fingers am I holding up?"

"Four," I answer quickly. "I can see the reflection in the TV."

He rolls his eyes. "Okay, how about this, I'm going to go outside and say something. Tell Logan to follow me, then he can tell you the message, and you can tell me."

I look over at Logan. He waves his hand. "Fine, but I'm not a side show freak you can use to amaze your friends."

"You're right, you aren't. You're an enormous pain in my ass that happens to need my help, so, get going. I'll wait here."

He nods.

"Okay, Carlos. Go for it," I say firmly.

He rises to his feet and storms out of my bedroom, shutting the door behind him. A few minutes later, he strides back in, Logan right behind him.

They both stand in front of me, Logan folds his

arms across his chest.

"Okay," Carlos says making a go ahead gesture with his hands.

I look over at Logan.

"First of all, he sang the chorus to Time Warp all the way across the street, then he said, ask not what you can do for your Carlos, but what your Carlos can do for you. Seriously. Where did you find this guy?"

I repeat the information to Carlos. The blood drains from his face.

"Look, Carlos, I know this is a lot to handle, okay? But I'm running out of time here and I need your help."

I quickly fill him in about The Reaper and about suspecting Becker of being the mystery boyfriend.

He takes a few deep breaths.

"So why does this Reaper want you?"

It's a really good question. My eyes flicker to Logan who shakes his head.

"We aren't sure."

"And you really think Becker would do something like that to Logan? To Kaylee?"

I shrug. "He's strong enough to take down Logan."

"If he took me by surprise," Logan retorts.

I roll my eyes. "*If he took him by surprise.* And Becker could have dragged his body onto the bridge and tossed it over."

"If he did, why do you think Kaylee didn't say something?"

"Maybe she was too scared. Maybe he threatened

her?"

Logan shakes his head. "No way. Kaylee was nothing if not a stone cold bitch. No way would she have let him scare her."

"Maybe she was in love with him?" Carlos says thoughtfully. "I mean, she was pregnant. Maybe she wanted him to dump Cassidy when she told him about the baby, but instead, he just killed her."

"Blackmail? Threatening to use a pregnancy to force him to be with her? That plays more like the Kaylee I knew," Logan says.

"Logan agrees."

Carlos perks up, looking proud to have someone validate his theory, even if it's someone he can't see or hear.

"So what's the next move?" Carlos asks, sitting down on the bed.

I look at Logan who nods.

"I'm taking Cassidy dress shopping for Homecoming tomorrow. I'm going to try to talk to her about it then. Maybe she knows something. If Kaylee was having a fling with Becker, maybe she threw it in Cassidy's face. That seems like something Kaylee would do."

"You should ask Carlos to talk to Becker."

"Forget it Logan."

"Forget what?" Carlos asks, looking confused.

"Logan thinks you should talk to Becker. But it's a terrible idea. If he is guilty, what do you think he'll do if he thinks Carlos is sniffing around? So like I said, forget it."

Carlos puts his hand on mine. "I will try to talk to him, if it'll help."

I shake my head. "Not no, but hell no Carlos, I mean it. Just let me deal with this. What you can do is use your incredible people skills to get close to Madison. She adores you and she was Kaylee's best friend. She says she didn't know about the guy, but she knew something, I'm sure. Just get her gossiping."

He nods, "That I can do."

I smile half-heartedly.

"Um, can you ask Logan to give us a minute alone? I want to talk to you privately for a minute."

I nod. "Scram Logan."

"Are you kidd—you know what? Fine. I'll be back later."

He vanishes and I lay back.

"He's gone."

Carlos lies beside me. "Ok, so I have to ask. Are you in love with Logan?"

I laugh dryly.

"Why would you ask that? I mean, he's dead."

Carlos snorts. "Yeah. I know that. But he's here, talking to you. You can see him. And you're helping him. But the last few weeks, you've been so…"

"Moody?" I offer.

"Not the word I was going for but, sure. We'll go with moody."

I sigh heavily. It feels like there's a ton of bricks on my chest and no matter what I do, I can't seem to lift the weight.

"Yeah. I am."

"And Bruno?"

"Maybe? God, this is all so messed up."

"Yeah, tell me about it."

I roll over, looking Carlos straight in the eye.

"I can't be in love with Logan. He makes me crazy. I literally want to punch him in the face half the time."

"But?"

"But the other half of the time, I just want to be near him."

"You realize there's no scenario in which this ends well, right?"

I lick my lips. "I know. I guess, I just want to hold onto him for as long as I can. But I know that eventually, I'm going to have to let him go."

"I'm so sorry, Zoe Bowie."

I nod. "I know. It just hurts so much."

I feel a teardrop escape the corner of my eye and I wipe it away quickly.

"And when you are hurt, you push people away. I know that, Zoe. Deep down, I think he probably does too. But, you should really try to just…set things straight with him. Let go of the pain and fear because at the end of the day, it's not how you want to remember your time with him."

"You are stupid smart with all the girly emotional

stuff, you know that? What the hell kind of man are you?" I chuckle sadly.

He's right. I know it. I need to set things right with Logan. Because our time together is quickly running out.

"So what do I do about Bruno, oh wise swami?"

He tucks his hand under my chin, "Do you care about Bruno?"

I nod.

"And he makes you feel?"

I sniffle. "Special. Loved. Safe."

He nods, "Then just let him love you, and love him as much as you can in return. Love him as much as you're able to right now. There's no shame in that."

I lean back. "You should consider a career as a therapist."

"I could have my own talk show."

"And you could make people cry on TV."

He tilts his head back, "I have always wanted to make people cry on TV."

A few hours later I'm picking at the last slice of cold, leftover pizza when Logan finally gets back.

"Where were you?" I ask, walking back to my bedroom with my plate and a two liter of Diet Dew tucked under my arm.

"I went to Becker's. I just, I dunno. I was trying to remember if it was his face, but it's still a big blank."

I close my door behind Logan. Mom's at work, but I still feel safer with the door shut, just in case.

"Don't beat yourself up. You've been traumatized.

It's only natural your mind would block pieces out to try to protect you. Especially if it was someone you knew."

He looks down at the floor. "I suppose."

He flops into my chair and I curl up on the floor at the end of my bed.

"Look Logan. I want to apologize."

"For what?" he asks, looking genuinely surprised.

"Oh, you know. For being my usual, crazy, bitchy self. I'm really sorry."

He looks up, holding my eyes. "It's alright Zoe. I understand. I know none of this has been easy on you either."

I lick my lips. "Yeah, but the thing is, I don't know how much time we have left together and I don't want to spend it like this, being angry and catty."

A rogue tear slides down my cheek before I can blink it away.

"I just want you to know, that I love you. And I'm going to miss you so much it feels like my heart is going to cave in."

I blow out a long breath. Logan is beside me in the blink of an eye, wiping the tears away.

"I think the reason I can do this, the reason I can be solid sometimes, is because of you. Because when I'm with you, I feel alive. More alive than I've felt in a really long time. But the longer I stay, the more I want to stay forever. And that isn't good for either of us," he says sadly.

I nod, leaning against him.

"I know. But it doesn't make it any easier."

"For me either, Zoe." He kisses the top of my head.

Then I feel myself start to slide through him, his firm skin replaced by cold air.

"It's just so unfair. We should have had time," I whine.

"We have right now. Maybe that's all we get. But I'm grateful for every second of it, I want you to know that."

I push the plate aside and climb into bed, patting the blanket next to me. Logan lies down beside me, his own eyes wet with tears.

"I didn't know ghosts could cry."

He frowns. "These are the manliest of tears. Reserved for things like toe stubbing and accidental snake bites to the buttocks."

I laugh through the tears and close my eyes, letting myself drift off to the sound of his breathing.

"And for letting go of you," he adds quietly.

Seventeen

MORNING COMES AND THIS TIME, when my alarm goes off, Logan is gone. Something inside me feels like a deep well, hollow and cold. I roll out of bed and shower quickly. Knowing I'm going to be trying on dresses later I opt for a soft white peasant dress and soft suede belt. I'm buckling the strap on my heels when Logan appears in my room.

"Sorry, I meant to be here when you woke up, but I lost track of time a little."

I shrug and proceed to weave my hair into a loose braid, tying it off with a bit of ribbon. Standing up I go to the jewelry box and pull it open. It's made of wood and brass and when I tug open the tiny glass doors, Brahms lullaby starts playing. A birthday gift from my father when I was a little girl. Now every time I hear the tune I feel close to him, and I really want to feel close to him today.

"Look what I found," I say, holding up a long silver chain with a bottle cap dangling from it.

Logan grins, walking over to see it better. "I can't believe you still have that."

"We were what, like six?"

He shakes his head. "And I gave it to you in exchange for—"

"A kiss. My first kiss as a matter of fact."

"And you kept it all this time?"

I shrug. "First kisses are a big deal for a girl."

I don't tell him that after he gave it to me, for the next few weeks, I'd convinced myself it meant we were married. I'd even told my dad that I was going to have to move out of the house and move into the tree house with Logan since he was my husband. Dad just laughed and told me that someday, I'd get married for real and when that happened, that he'd have to approve of it because he'd be giving away his only daughter.

I feel my heart stutter at the memory.

"It was a big deal for me too."

I roll my eyes. "Whatever Logan. You probably don't even remember—"

He holds out a finger. "You were wearing a yellow sweater. I told you it made you look like a bumble bee. You hit me. And then, I gave you the necklace because you were crying. You sniffled and said, *what does it cost?* And I said," he pauses so I finish.

"*A kiss from a crying girl.*"

"See? I remember."

I smile sadly. Why can't life ever turn out the way it's supposed to?

Putting the necklace over my head I let it fall against my chest. I don't look back at Logan until I've fought back the tears. I'm not going to cry again. Not today. Today, I just have to... survive.

"Look, about Bruno," Logan starts, clearing his throat. "It's okay for you to like him. I mean, not that you need permission, but...Bruno's a good guy. You deserve a good guy."

I take a deep breath.

"Okay, quit trying to make me cry, you freaking sap. I just did my mascara."

He looks offended, then realizes that I'm teasing.

"Me? You busted out with the childhood memories. Geeze woman. Pining away much?"

I chuckle. "Well, you know me. I never throw away perfectly good jewelry."

He lowers his voice seriously. "You look beautiful, by the way. Just thought you should know."

I pull my shoulder into my chin. "Oh, I know. But thanks just the same. Are we ready to do this?"

He nods and I hear the doorbell ring. I'd almost forgotten I asked Bruno for a ride today since I was going shopping with Cassidy right after school.

"Um, I'm going to go hang out at my house today, okay? I want to see my mom, make sure she's doing alright."

I nod. "See you at lunch?"

He smiles and vanishes.

By the time I get to the front door my mom

is chatting away with Bruno, who looks completely undaunted by her. Granted she's only five foot four, a hundred pounds wet, but she can be as intimidating as a grizzly bear.

I kiss her quickly on the cheek, pushing Bruno out the door with a hand to his chest.

"Bye mom. See you later," I say, ushering him toward the truck.

"What, you don't want me to talk to your mom?"

I roll my eyes. "I don't want her to start sending out our wedding invitations just yet. She tends to get a little over excited."

He opens my door, stopping to kiss me before he lets me in. I sigh deeply. I really do enjoy kissing Bruno.

"She's nice," he says.

"Um, she's meaner than a bag full of squirrels and twice as nuts."

He laughs.

"What's so funny?" I ask.

He turns the key in the ignition. "You. I don't think I've heard you insult anybody in a few days. Are you saving up for a special occasion?"

Now it's my turn to laugh. "Maybe. It's almost Homecoming after all."

"Good. I like to watch you get all wrath-y. Just, you know, not on me."

I smile until may face hurts.

When we get to school Bruno walks me to my locker as usual, only he's acting weird, jumpy.

"What got sprinkled on your granola today?" I ask, turning the combination lock.

He steps back and when I open the locker it's full of flowers. Not roses or carnations or anything as mundane as that, but it's full of tall, white daisies.

I pull out the bouquet and inhale deeply. I love daisies. They're my favorite flowers.

"How did you know?" I ask, already suspecting the answer.

Carlos walks up from behind, his hand in the air.

"He called in back up last night."

I stare at Bruno. "When did you have time to put these in here?"

He shrugs meekly, "I got up early and did it this morning."

"Then you came all the way back to my house to pick me up?"

I'm so stunned, I'm not even sure what to say when he grins sheepishly. Looking back down at the flowers I see a little card tucked into the flowers. Pulling it out I read it.

For the prettiest girl I've ever met.
Love,
Kyle.

It's so strange to see that he's signed his first name it takes a second to click in. For as long as I have known him, everyone just called him Bruno. I never even thought to ask if he would prefer something else.

Stepping in close I wrap my arms around his neck. "Thanks, Kyle. I love them."

He blushes wildly and I reach onto my tiptoes to kiss him. The bell rings, jarring us apart.

He brushes his hand over my hair, kissing me on the jaw.

"See you at lunch."

Coach Mason stops me after first period to give me a list of the teachers chaperoning for the dance.

"Thanks. I'll pass this onto the Dance Committee," I say tucking it in my bag.

He tilts his head, looking at me quizzically. "Is everything alright Zoe? I can't help but notice you seem a little distracted lately."

I frown. "No, everything is good. Why? Are my grades slipping?"

"No, I just noticed, you seem to have come into a new group of friends this year."

"Yeah," I say, trying not to sound irritated at his keeping me so late. "They're great."

"You know, we have grief counselors available to students still struggling with what happened to Kaylee."

Okay, this is just getting weird. Am I sending off some kind of pathetic, crazy chick vibes? Or worse, had he somehow overheard me talking to Logan yesterday after class? God, he probably thinks I was talking to myself.

"Thanks. I'll keep that in mind," I say with a smile and rush out of the room.

As soon as I step foot in the hallway, my group of friends are there waiting. The girls are all taking turns cooing over the flowers and the guys are giving Bruno—no Kyle—a hard time.

I turn to my poor, embarrassed boyfriend and plant a kiss on him.

"So, I was thinking, I know everyone calls you Bruno, but would it be okay if I just call you Kyle from now on?"

I ask loudly, making sure the rest of the group hears me.

He smiles. "Sure, if you want."

He bends over, plants a kiss on the tip of my nose and leads me out to his truck.

I don't see Logan at lunch, which worries me more that I'd like to admit. We opt to skip the pizza today for Chinese and I'm glad we do. Any more pizza and I'm not going to be able to squeeze myself into that red dress anymore.

"So, what do you have going on tonight?" Bruno asks as the waitress hands out our plates.

"I'm kidnapping her," Cassidy says with a mischievous grin.

Bruno glances over at me and I bat my eyelashes

innocently. He sighs. "As long as you bring her back."

"Where are you two going?" Becca asks curiously.

I glance up at Cassidy, who is looking at me like she's trying to swallow the giant foot in her mouth. I give her a subtle nod.

"Dress shopping for Homecoming," she answers, stuffing a fork full of rice in her mouth.

Becca stares at her silently, her face surprised.

"Do you want to come?" I ask, an open invitation to the table. It's kind of a hollow gesture since I know for a fact that she, Madison and the twins have cheer practice tonight.

"I'll go," Darla chimes in, making me almost choke on my noodles.

I force a smile. "Great. Meet us after school."

Just what I need, a two hour car ride with my new boyfriend's jilted ex. Then again, maybe I can use her to my advantage.

There's no reason to think the day could get any better. Logan still hasn't shown up, I've been accosted twice by grief counselors trying to convince me to come share my feelings about Kaylee, and mom frantically texted me when the police showed up at our door with a search warrant for the necklace I already told them they could come get. I sigh deeply, watching from my desk, as the final minutes of last period tick away.

Beside me, Leena taps her pencil on the edge of her desk impatiently. The sound makes my eyeball twitch as I fight the urge to lean over, rip the pencil out of her hand and shove it up her—

The bell rings and I'm out of my desk like a shot, homicidal thoughts float away as I step into the hallway and see Bruno already waiting for me. He's leaning against the lockers, twisting the lacrosse stick in his hands absently as he chats with Becker. The impulse to walk over and push my way between them is strong, making me wonder at what point I'd already decided on his guilt. Maybe it isn't fair. But the sight of them together, laughing, makes my skin crawl. Luckily, before I can charge over and make a scene like a neurotic freak, Cassidy walks over, folding herself into Becker's arms. He hugs her tightly and lowers his head to kiss her. My stomach lurches.

Then Bruno catches sight of me and holds out his free hand, which I take without hesitation, letting him draw me against him.

"Hey. How was class?" He asks warmly.

I swallow hard. The decision to tell him the truth was sort of made for me. In a town this small, no secret stays buried for long.

Lowering my voice I whisper, "I need to talk to you for a minute. Privately."

He nods, his face going from joy to abject fear in a matter of seconds. We cross the hall and I pull him into

Mr. Mason's empty room, closing the door behind us.

"I need to tell you something," I begin slowly. He takes a seat on the corner of Mr. Mason's oak desk.

I straighten my shoulders, squaring off to him, my arms folded across my chest. "The police came to my house today. They had a search warrant."

I wait for him to say something, trying to gauge his reaction carefully. His expression falls, then recovers quickly, a smile lighting up his face.

"Zoe, you scared the living shit out of me."

I feel my eyebrows crease. "What?"

He hops off the desk, locking his arms around my waist. "I thought you were dumping me."

"Why would I do that? Never mind. It doesn't matter. But seriously, the police questioned me about Kaylee's murder because I had been up at The Tower and they found my blood—"

He holds up a hand. "Blood?"

I hold out my palm. The scratch is deep and still ugly, but I'd taken the bandage off and never put another one on.

"I was up there after Logan..." I let my words trail off, choosing my story very carefully. "I went up there to try to make sense of what happened to Logan. It was way before Kaylee was killed. But I cut myself on The Tower and they found my blood, so they thought—"

"They thought you might have something to do with it."

I nod, clutching my hand. "But I didn't. I swear

to God I didn't."

He reaches out and touches the side of my face. "I know that Zoe."

"You do?"

He nods, leaning forward he kisses me gently. "No one who threatens to kill people as often as you do would be dumb enough to *actually* kill someone."

I smile against his lips.

"You," he whispers. "For all your tough talk, you have a very gooey center."

I pull away just a little. "I wouldn't go that far."

He just shakes his head. "You might be able to hide it from everyone else, but I've seen it. Do you remember last year when Kaylee was tormenting that freshman girl with the red hair?"

How could I forget? The girl, not knowing any better, had accidentally taken Kaylee's parking space. Kaylee had tracked the girl down before class and shut her long red hair in a locker. The girl was in tears. Kaylee and the lemmings just laughed.

That was the day I got myself on Kaylee's bitch radar. She never retaliated against me, but I spent the better part of the year jumping at shadows waiting for her to take her revenge.

Now that I think about it, I can't help but wonder if Logan had somehow tempered her rage on my behalf. I make a mental note to ask him about it later.

I nod.

"I'll never forget it. You walked right up to Kaylee

and told her to go *take a Midol and get the fuck over it.* Then you picked the lock and got that girl out."

My mouth twitches. "She transferred to private school like two weeks later."

"But you, you were this fierce, amazing, beautiful creature. An avenging angel. That's when I saw you, really saw you, for the first time. I think I fell for you that day."

"And yet you waited all this time to make your move on me."

He rolls his eyes. "Well, you weren't usually what I'd call approachable."

I frown. He's right and it's no one's fault but my own.

"I'm working on that," I say honestly.

He grins. "Don't work too hard."

I sigh, knowing we've gotten way off track.

"But, like I was saying, while I was there I found her necklace. I brought it home. I was going to have it fixed and give it back to her." I sigh deeply. "I knew Logan would want her to have it."

"See? Gooey center."

I lower my chin and give him a *be serious* look.

He hugs me. "Zoe, we were all questioned about Kaylee. Me included. I'm not worried about it."

"But people talk and when they find out that the police searched my house—"

He shrugs. "People will talk. Then they will find whoever actually did this, and they will talk about that."

I lean against him, resting my head in the curve

of his neck. "You don't care that people will be talking about me?"

"Are you kidding? People are talking about you now. I swear it's like they never knew you existed before and now, you're like the resident superstar. Not to brag, but most of the guys on the team are just waiting for us to break up so they can have a shot at you. But they are going to be waiting a hell of a long time."

"Yes, they are. Besides, I doubt any one of them could handle the massive amount of crazy that comes with dating me."

"Speaking of crazy, do you have any plans Friday night?"

I press my hands against his chest, feeling his strong, steady heartbeat under my fingers.

"Why? Are you thinking we should knock over a bank or something?"

He tilts his head back and forth, like he's considering it. "I was thinking about something a little more benign. Like dinner and a movie?"

I grab the collar of his shirt, "This is very important, Kyle. It could decide the very fate of our relationship." Lowering my chin, I look up at him seriously, "Romantic comedy or bloody zombie flick?"

He raises one eyebrow. "Zombies for sure."

I grin. "Correct. Looks like it's going to be smooth sailing from here."

He kisses my nose, "Good to hear. But I gotta go. I'm already late for practice."

I sigh and release him. "Fine, go if you must. I have to go meet up with Cassidy and Darla anyway."

He cringes. "About Darla."

I fold my arms across my chest.

"Whatever she tells you, just…take it with a grain of salt, okay?"

"Why? Does she know all your deep, dark secrets?"

He rolls his eyes. "No, but she's still a little bitter."

"Darla? Bitter? Surely you jest."

"It's an extreme case."

I shrug. "Every female has the batshit crazy gene. It just takes that special guy to activate it. Sounds like you were the lucky dude."

He frowns and I wave him away. "Relax. Go to practice. I can handle Darla and her bitterness."

He nods and walks out. I'm about to follow him when Logan flashes in.

"Are you okay?" He asks, breathlessly.

I frown. "Yeah, why?"

"The police came to my house today. They were asking my mom a lot of questions about you."

"Me?"

He nods. "They think we were in a secret relationship or something. Then they searched your house. They didn't find anything but…"

"But what?"

"It's going to look bad, Zoe. Them asking questions like that, then searching your house. When people find out, they are going to assume you're involved."

"The police can't find anything to tie me to Kaylee, because there isn't anything to find."

"I know that. And even if the police never press charges, just being a suspect will put you under a microscope in the worst way."

"I know. I just told Bruno about it."

"What did you tell him?"

I shrug. "The truth. Minus the part where I can see and talk to his recently deceased best friend." I bite my bottom lip. "All we can do is figure out whose car you saw that night. If I can figure out who killed you, maybe I can make all this go away."

He nods. Reaching out he touches my arm, solid only for a moment before fading into air.

"Logan, you have to keep trying to remember what happened. I'll follow the car lead, but it's all just such a long shot. And even once you remember, we will have to figure out how to get the police on board."

"I thought about that. They never found my cell phone. It was turned off so they couldn't trace it. But I know where it is. I lost it that night, it fell in this hollow spot at the base of a tree. If we can find the phone, plant it on the killer. Then all it will take is an anonymous phone call."

I nod. "That's a good plan actually."

"You sound surprised."

"Color me impressed is all. In the mean time, I have a shopping date with the girls."

"You want back up?"

I almost laugh. "So you can hang out in the dressing rooms in Niemen? No thanks perv."

He folds his arms indignantly. "Fine. I'll be here, watching TV in your room."

I lick my lips, "Actually, could you do something for me?"

He tilts his head. I want to kick myself for even asking, but deep in the pit of my stomach guilt and worry gnaw at me.

"Can you keep an eye on Bruno? He's at practice with Becker and…I'm just worried about him."

His jaw clenches and he nods. "You really care about him, don't you?"

God, is this feeling ever going to go away? Every time Logan and I are together it feels like I'm slowly bleeding to death from a million tiny cuts.

"I do."

He looks away, trying to conceal the pain in his expression, but failing. It stabs me in the heart like a knife.

"So do I," he whispers and vanishes.

Eighteen

THE DRIVE IS LONG AND LOUD. I take shotgun leaving Darla in the back seat. She leans forward, head poking out between us as she recounts her latest drama.

"Can you believe Peter asked me out?" Her voice is dry, tone appalled.

"Pete is a nice guy," I defend. Though, to be frank, I would never go out with him either. Not because he isn't attractive or because he has all the humor of an impacted tooth, but because I'm not convinced he doesn't have some sort of weird fetish. He seems like the type. All proper and buttoned up on the outside, total freak behind closed doors.

She snorts, reading my expression. "He is nice. Hannibal Lector was nice until he started eating people's faces off."

I laugh, I know I shouldn't, but I can't help myself. I had always wondered what a guy like Bruno was doing with a chick like Darla, but now I sort of get it. He just likes loud, obnoxious, ballsy women. I'm actually kind of perfect for him. But that makes me even more curious about their break up.

"Okay, this may totally suck of me, but I have to ask. Why did you and Kyle break up?"

Darla presses her lips into a hard line, glaring at me.

From the driver's seat Cassidy laughs dryly.

"Are you kidding? You don't know?"

I turn back to Darla, feeling like I missed the punch line.

"I have no clue. That's why I asked."

"Well, it's really none of your damn business, is it?"

"Get over it Darla, everyone else knows."

"He dumped me. He told me he didn't want to waste his time with me anymore."

I raise one eyebrow. "That doesn't sound like the Kyle I know."

She sits back in her seat, pulling her legs up under her.

"Well, you don't really know him at all, do you?" She looks out the window. "Don't worry, one day he'll do the same thing to you and you won't even see it coming. Then you'll know who he really is."

"Pull over the bitterness bus, Darla. It's time to get off," Cassidy says from the front seat. I don't think I've ever heard her talk to someone like that before.

But, it just proves Darla's point. I don't really know Cassidy, or Becker or Kyle for that matter.

"Bruno's a great guy. Don't listen to her. She's still hurt that he broke up with her."

At the risk of pissing off the only person in the car not hating on me, I decide to bring up Becker.

I toss my hair over my shoulder and smile at Cassidy. "So…you and Becker? You guys seem so happy."

She shrugs. "Yeah. He has his moments. But we're good."

"I think you guys should go out for Homecoming King and Queen. I'll nominate you," I offer sweetly.

She glances over at me, looking confused. "Why would you do that?"

I shrug. "It's like you said. I want a perfect couple to look up to. I mean, things are great with Kyle." From the back seat Darla snorts. "But you guys have been together longer and it looks like you are inseparable."

"That's not what I heard," Darla chimes in from the back seat.

"Shut up Darla," Cassidy commands, her face flushing.

I look over my shoulder at Darla in the back seat. Maybe bringing her was a lucky break.

"What do you mean?" I ask as innocently as possible.

She looks only too pleased to rub her words in Cassidy's face.

"I mean, sweet innocent Cassidy had a bit of a fling this summer, didn't you?"

In the front seat Cassidy sucks in a deep breath,

her cheeks flaring red. "It's not a big deal."

"My ass it's not a big deal." Darla leans forward, "If you can air my dirty laundry, yours is fair game too, sweetie."

Cassidy clears her throat. "I got drunk at Bruno's party and made out with another guy."

I let my eyes widen in surprise. "What guy?"

She glances over quickly before locking her eyes back on the road. "Not Bruno if that's what you're thinking."

"It was Logan," Darla answers, her voice breathy. "Can't blame her for that one really, I mean, what girl wouldn't want to make out with him? He was gorgeous."

"And funny," Cassidy adds.

"And sweet."

I roll my eyes, "And a total pain in the ass, as I recall."

They just laugh.

"So, how did Becker take it?"

Cassidy frowns, "Oh, he was pissed, of course. But I told him I was so blitzed I thought Logan was him."

"And he bought that?" Darla asks before I can.

"Sure. Boys are really stupid, and I think in a weird way he was sort of flattered."

I pucker, looking out the window. "Yeah, weird."

"It was moot anyway. Becker used to hang on Logan's every word; he had some sort of idol complex I think. Becker never would have blamed Logan. Kaylee, on the other hand…"

Darla laughs. "Please. She was already cheating on him by then. She didn't give a rat's ass."

I flip around in my seat.

"Cheating on him with who?" Darla glares at me suspiciously. "I mean, it would kind of be like cheating on Channing Tatum with David Spade, right?"

Darla relaxes, "Who knows? She kept it under pretty tight wraps. But, she said something about it once, do you remember, Cassidy? At that sleep over?"

"Oh, yeah. She said she found someone who really understood her. We asked who it was and she just told us *he isn't some stupid high school boy.*"

"Yeah, I always figured it was one of those baseball players who comes in for the summer. But then, when school started, she was still acting weird. Breaking up with Logan and stuff."

"You knew about that?" I ask quickly.

"She told Madison. Madison told me."

I break into a grin. "Wow, remind me never to tell you gossipy bitches anything."

Cassidy glances over to make sure I'm joking. I stick my tongue out at her. She laughs and Darla joins in.

Thing is, I'm not joking at all.

It seems unfair that I still have to go through with the actual shopping portion of the evening now that I've gotten the info I came for, but it ends up actually being kind of fun. We make our way through three stores, trying on the biggest, ugliest gowns we can find. Cassidy snaps pics of me in the various dresses and sends them to Bruno. He responds with a series of thumbs down images.

Then, I try on a bubble gum pink taffeta gowns that makes me look like a spool of cotton candy and send a picture to Bruno with the message, *how about this one?*

His response is a very simple, *only if you want to embarrass yourself by showing up in the same outfit as me.*

Three stores and two and a half hours later we hit a little boutique I've never seen before. In the window is the most amazing dress I've ever seen. It's silver with a sheer black lace overlay, fitted to the body, a slight v neck front with lace that rolls over the shoulder and down the back. It's short, shorter than anything I've ever worn before, but not so short that it looks slutty. It's edgy and sexy and dark. And I love it immediately.

Cassidy sees me eyeing it.

"Oh yeah, that's the dress. Go try it on."

She ushers me into the shop and leads me to the dressing room, ordering the sales clerk to bring one in my size.

It fits perfectly. Cassidy holds up her phone to snap a pic and Darla covers it with her hand.

"Nope. A dress like that deserves the element of surprise."

I glance at the tag, bracing myself for sticker shock only to find it pretty reasonable. Reasonable enough that I snag a new strapless bra to go with it.

"Bruno isn't going to know what hit him," Cassidy says wistfully.

Cassidy decides on a pale pink long gown with beading along the bodice, and Darla goes for a simple green velvet dress with a 70's vibe. The drive home seems to go faster, and I let myself relax and just enjoy the company. I've never had girlfriends, unless you count Carlos, and it's kind of nice. Even though I couldn't care less about 90 per cent of the things they are talking about, it's fun just to listen to them go on about makeup and celebrities, and my personal favorite, how long you should go between hair colorings.

It's chatter, white noise in the back of my head. I just let them talk, I doubt I would have anything of value to add anyway.

By the time Cassidy drops me off it's almost eleven and mom is waiting for me at the door, her eyes blood shot.

I'd texted her about my plans, but I'd failed to realize how long the adventure would take. The last thing I thought was that she'd wait up for me.

"That was a long trip," she says, closing the door behind me. Logan is sitting on the couch, watching TV.

"She was worried," he says without turning around to look at me. "Don't be mean to her. She didn't have to wait up for you."

He's right. I know he spent most of the day with his own mom, who is probably suffering in ways I can't even imagine. I look at my mother, really look at her for the first time in months. Maybe years. Her curly hair is frizzed out, she has dark circles under her eyes and her skin is pale, too pale.

It takes me a minute to realize that Logan is right. I've been mean to her. Not intentionally, not really. But after dad died, I sort of decided not to allow myself to rely on anyone anymore, including her. She probably expected me to lean on her for support, but I'd done just the opposite. I learned not to lean on anyone. And being with Logan has also reminded me how short life can be. If something happened to one of us tomorrow, how would I want to have left things?

I smile. "I'm glad you're still up. Kyle asked me to Homecoming, and I said yes."

She almost melts with relief. I lead her into the kitchen.

"Look," I say, pulling the dress out of the bag covering it.

She sighs softly. "It's beautiful. So grown up."

I fold the dress over my arm. "The thing is mom, I know I haven't been as…available as you'd like. I'm sorry about that. I've had stuff and that's not an excuse but—"

She holds up her hand. "Zoe, I understand. I haven't exactly been around either. But it has sort of felt like you were pushing me away. Like, you didn't need me anymore."

She sits down at the table. "When we lost your dad, we lost each other too."

I sit down beside her. "I know. But I just want you to know that I love you. And I want you to be a part of what's going on in my life." I pause. "A very silent part."

She chuckles. "Deal."

Leaning forward I hug her. I can feel her shake with quiet tears so I hold on a little longer.

When she lets go she wipes her eyes. "So, you and Kyle. Is it official?"

I nod. "Yeah it is."

"And he treats you well?"

I nod again. I can see the top of Logan's head through the arch way.

"He does."

"Are you in love with him?"

I stare at her, my heart taking off like a rocket in my chest. "The truth is, I fell in love with somebody else a long time ago. I haven't really gotten over that yet."

She smiles sadly. "I understand. When I think about your dad, I can't imagine ever loving anyone else like that ever again. But I think we both have to remember, we can always love the people we lose, it doesn't mean we can never love again. I think it will just be a different love. But it doesn't betray them or their memory. They would want us to be happy."

I swallow back salty tears. I know she's right. Logan has told me as much.

"Then why does it hurt so much?" I ask, my voice small and quiet.

She holds me again, stroking my hair.

"Because things have to hurt before they can heal."

Logan is sitting in my chair when I finish catching mom up on my new social status and go to bed. I feel the tension melt out of my neck and shoulders at the sight of him.

"Hey," I say softly, closing my door.

"Hey. I take it shopping went well."

I nod, hanging the dress, bag and all in my closet.

"Yeah. I don't think Becker is our guy. Cassidy says he wasn't bent out of shape about what happened. He wasn't angry with you at all. She actually said he was kind of flattered, which is just weird."

"So do you think we should check out Jesus?"

I roll my eyes. "If Jesus killed you I'll eat my own arm. That guy is a big teddy bear."

"You are probably right about that. But he's sort of our last lead."

I flop down onto my bed. "I know. But the girls told me Kaylee's mystery guy doesn't even go to our school. I think we might be at a dead end. Unless you remembered something?"

He shakes his head.

Sitting back against the headboard I rub my eyes with my thumbs.

"So what do we do now?" I ask wearily.

"I'm going to keep tabs on the investigation, make sure they aren't seriously considering you as a suspect.

And I'll keep trying to remember what happened."

"What about me?"

He smiles. "You just keep being your charming self."

I pull the pillow out from behind me and stuff it over my face.

"I have a date with Kyle on Friday." I say, my voice muffled by the feathers.

"I know."

Pulling the pillow away I shoot him a look.

"How do you know?"

"He mentioned it to Becker tonight. They hung out at Bruno's house after practice. I was with him all night. I saw the pictures you sent him. It looked like you were having fun."

His voice is light, but his face is sad.

I shrug. "Yeah. I kind of did. Why were you at his house so late?"

He rolls his eyes. "Because you asked me to keep an eye on him, remember? I stayed until Becker left."

Oh yeah. I'd almost forgotten.

"Thanks for doing that," I manage weakly. Thank you doesn't seem like enough, not nearly enough. But it's all I've got at the moment.

"I don't think I can stay here anymore," he says out of nowhere.

I jerk to attention.

"Why not?"

He looks at me, smiling weakly.

"It's just too hard. I'll stay outside. Keep an eye out for The Reaper."

I bite my bottom lip. "But you don't want to be near me anymore."

He shakes his head. "Don't say it like that, Zoe. It's just too painful."

I laugh dryly. "Yes, because it's just a walk in the park for me."

He stands up, stuffing his hands in his pockets.

"Yeah, well you don't have to stand by and watch the person you love falling in love with someone else."

And with that he vanishes, leaving me stunned and speechless, feeling like he just carved my heart out of my chest with a dull spoon.

Ninteen

THE NEXT FEW DAYS ROLL BY in a disturbing wave of normalcy. The first week of school is over and, as Cassidy expected, Kyle and I are nominated for Homecoming King and Queen.

All of that I can deal with. But it's going home at night, the driving, painful ache that throbs through me every time I close my eyes. Every once in a while I catch a glimpse of Logan, across the street or down the hall. But he doesn't speak to me anymore. He just turns away.

And slowly, the hole in my heart fills with rage. I lie awake at night thinking of all the things I will say to him when I see him again. About how I will call him a coward and a liar. But deep down, I just don't want the pain to stop. I don't want to get over him. And despite my best efforts not to, Logan is right. I'm falling for Kyle.

He picks me up a little before six. Mom is already at work, but she wants details. Yeah, I'll get right on that.

Pulling open the door I see that Kyle has his back to me, looking across the street like he sees something.

For one insane, frantic moment I think he might see Logan. But when I follow his gaze, there's nothing.

"Hey," I say drawing him back to me.

He turns, holding out his hand. There's a tiny blue box nestled in his palm.

"What's that?" I ask suspiciously.

He chuckles. "A gift. For our first official date. Open it."

My curiosity overwhelms me as I take the box, backing up so he can come inside. Lifting the lid I see a tiny pearl on a silver chain.

"It's beautiful." I say, staring at the white jewel. "You didn't have to do that."

He takes it from my fingers, motioning for me to turn around.

"I got it in Hawaii. I went last summer with Logan and his family. We went diving and there was this bed of oysters. We picked some to eat, and this was inside one."

He clasps it around my neck and I touch it gently where it lies in the hollow of my neck.

Turning around I throw my arms around his neck with more vigor than I mean to, nearly knocking him over.

"Thank you," I whisper, clutching him tightly.

Obviously he doesn't get my emotional response—how could he?—but he hugs me back tightly, lifting me off my feet.

When he sets me down. I'm somewhat recovered. I grab my tan jacket and we head out to his truck.

"So which dress did you decide on," he asks as we drive.

I laugh. "Oh, that's going to be a surprise."

He smiles. "Well, don't I need to know what color it is so we can match?"

I stare at him like he's speaking Greek.

"Huh?"

He shifts in his seat. "Oh. That was a thing with Darla. She always made me get a bow tie to match her dress color."

I laugh out loud and raise my right hand, "I solemnly promise never, under any circumstance, to make you dress to match me."

He shakes his head. "Sorry. I didn't mean to compare you, I thought it was just a chick thing. Kaylee used to do the same thing to Logan. I figured it was in the manual."

I grab his arm. "Are you telling me there are *instructions*? My god, I never got the memo. How have I lived my life without it?"

"Oh, I think you've done pretty well for yourself."

I grin and bring my shoulder to my chin playfully.

"Well, I did manage to land you, so I can't be doing too terrible."

He smiles brightly.

"Okay, I have to ask though. What the hell happened with you and Darla? Because, as you warned me, she is still hella bitter about it."

"You really want to know?"

I try to look uninterested and fail miserably.

"Yes. I know it is none of my business and you can totally plead the fifth and I won't hold it against you but, you just seem so…"

"Oh, this can't be good."

"Mellow. Like, easy to be around. I MUST know what she did to make you dump her. Otherwise, how will I know where the line is?"

"What line?"

"The line of how insane and bitchy I can be before you've had it with me."

He shakes his head. "Well, trust me, I doubt you could ever even get close to that line. But if you really want to know, I wasn't trying to be a jerk. But I realized that she wasn't the person for me. Like, I felt it in my heart. I liked her, and that was great. But I never fell in love with her. And I thought she deserved to be with someone who did."

"Wait, that's it? You dumped her because you weren't in love with her?"

He tilts his head. "Not just that. I realized I *never would* fall in love with her. She was a friend. But nothing more. What kind of relationship is that?"

I stare at him. He looks over warily.

"What?" he asks.

I lean my head against the seat.

"Wow. That's the most incredibly honest thing I've ever heard of. I knew you were amazing, but that might actually push you over the edge into perfect territory."

He laughs dryly. "No one's perfect Zoe."

"I didn't mean perfect, perfect. I meant perfect for me," I add quietly.

We descend upon the Captain's Table—the nicest restaurant in town—hand in hand. He made a reservation sparing us the nearly two hour wait at the door. As we make our way to the corner table, the dim area aglow by candle light, my heart crawls into my throat. Dinner, sure. Pizza. Tacos. But this, this is downright *romantic*. Not what I was expecting and I'm not entirely sure I'm ready for this. Two tables over my next door neighbor and her husband are staring at me as I take a seat. Three tables behind Kyle a couple in their late 80's or so are pointing to us and smiling in that vaguely condescending way only old people can. I scoot my chair in, folding my hands in my lap and cracking my knuckles.

"Are you alright?" Kyle asks, handing me the linen menu.

I plaster on a fake smile. This place probably cost him a month's worth of paychecks, what kind of terrible person would I be to complain about it? One of the things I've always liked about the dark haired boy is his salt of the earth demeanor. Sure, his family is obscenely wealthy, sure his house is the size of a football field. But he has a job, a truck he paid for himself, and I doubt he shops anywhere fancier than the local mall. This place is so far out of my comfort zone I can feel myself about to break out into hives.

"I've never been here before," I say honestly.

He grins meekly. "Yeah, I don't come here much myself. But the food is good and Mario, the owner, comes into the shop to get his oil changed. He's always telling me to come sometime, so I gave him a call and he got us in."

I feel myself relax just a little.

"That's cool."

"Yeah. I have all the best hookups," he says with a sarcastic laugh.

"Lucky you."

I pick up the menu, trying not to frown at the prices. The waiter makes his way over and we order.

"So," I fold my hands under my chin, elbows on the table. "What are your big plans for after High School?"

He takes a drink of water before answering. "College. I have scholarship offers from a few places. I'm leaning towards William & Mary."

I tilt my head. "You want to stay that close?"

He half shrugs. "I don't know yet. I'm keeping my options open."

"Always a good plan."

"What about you?"

I lean back. "I want to take a gap year. Travel, do some charity work. Then I'm off to NYU. I want to major in Anthropology and minor in Ancient Civilizations."

"So, you want to be Tomb Raider?"

I laugh, nearly choking on my water.

"More like Indiana Jones. Less guns, more whips."

"I think you would look great with a whip."

I tilt my glass. "Why thank you."

At that moment I see someone moving toward me out the corner of my eye. It's Logan. As soon as I see him he begins frantically motioning for me to follow him.

"Sorry, I need to use the bathroom. Be right back," I mumble, excusing myself from the table.

As soon as I'm out of earshot I mutter at Logan under my breath.

"This had better be important."

"It is," he assures me, following me to the bathroom.

I push open the door, thank heavens it's a one stall, and lock the door behind me.

"Get in here," I whisper and Logan appears beside me.

"What is it? Did you remember something?"

He shakes his head. "No, I was at your house, just sort of keeping an eye on things. But that Reaper showed up."

"Well, lucky for me, I wasn't there."

"No, you don't understand. It got out of your mom's car. It was with her."

I blink, trying to process his words.

"Is she alright? Did it try to…? I don't know, reap her?"

"No. It just followed her inside. And I followed it. It went into your room and just hovered there, like it was waiting for you. I told it to leave. I even tried to grab it—"

"That was stupid. You need to stay away from it Logan, I mean it."

"Not really the point. The point is, it said something."

I lean against the sink. "What did it say?"

"It said, *it's Zoe*."

I go from mildly upset to completely freaked out in no time flat. I stomp around, practically slamming myself into the walls, fingers pulling at my own hair.

Why does this thing want me? Why am I so special? None of this makes any sense. Logan keeps reaching out to grab me but he can't seem to make himself solid enough to make contact. I wave him off.

"We need to get you out of here, Zoe. Get you some place safe."

I look over at Logan. He looks as frazzled as I feel.

"Where exactly? Where is safe Logan? I can't hide from something that can walk through walls and make itself appear at will anywhere, any time."

Then a really terrifying thought hits me like a kick to the stomach. Mom. It followed my mom. What if it decides that sticking close to her is the best way to get to me? What if it hurts her? I can't even—

I blow out a deep breath, forcing the air from my lungs and purse my lips.

"It won't try anything here, in public."

"You don't know that Zoe. It very well could."

I shake my head. "Nah. If it wanted me that badly,

it could have taken me any time. Whatever it wants, whatever it's going to do, it won't be out in the open like this."

He rolls his eyes. "Just because you want that to be true doesn't mean—"

I spin on him, my finger poking where his chest would be if he were solid.

"What are you doing here anyway? I thought all this was too hard for you? Didn't you decide to bail on me?"

He steps back, an expression of real hurt flashing in his eyes.

"Zoe, I never left you. I wouldn't do that. I just couldn't keep pretending things could work between us. It isn't fair to either of us, you know that."

I poke him again.

"I don't want your excuses. And you don't get to bail on me like a coward and then come running to my rescue when it suits you. Just leave me alone."

With that I open the door and walk briskly back to my seat. I can feel him following me, but I ignore him.

"We need to go, Zoe." Logan says behind me.

I take my seat, not looking his way.

"So, a gap year. What kind of travel do you want to do?" Kyle asks, breaking off a chunk of bread and handing it to me.

"Oh, you know. Turkey. Greece. Egypt."

"Not the safest travel destinations," he says absently.

I nod. "True, but there's more to life than playing it safe, don't you think?"

"Zoe, please," Logan begs.

Kyle smirks. "You sound like Logan."

I almost spit my soda on him. Coughing into my napkin I manage to recover.

"What do you mean?"

Kyle looks up from his empty plate, motioning to the room around us.

"It's this thing Logan used to say. He said, 'If you aren't living life like there's no tomorrow, you're just wasting time.' It was one of his many philosophies. They all had the same basic theme. Get busy living or get busy dying."

I take a long drink of the soda, wishing it was something a little stronger.

"That sounds like Logan."

"Yeah, and look where it got me," he mutters.

Kyle looks away, his face faltering around the edges.

"You really miss him, huh?" I ask, reaching across the table to take his hand.

He nods, turning back to me.

"You know, I think Logan sent you to me."

I feel myself twitch just a little, drawing my hand away.

"Why do you say that?"

"Yeah, why does he say that?" Logan interjects.

Kyle shakes his head. "It sounds crazy when I say

it out loud."

I sit back in my chair, wringing my cloth napkin in my lap.

"It's not crazy. I feel Logan around me all the time," I admit softly. "Like he's still here."

Kyle tips his head to the side, looking at me with a gentle expression.

"When my dad died, I used to see him everywhere, all the time. Then after a while, I'd forget he was gone. I'd open my door and expect to see him. It's the same with Logan. Sometimes I can hear him, making a snide comment or telling me not to do something stupid. Not that I listen," I say with a half smile.

"Does it ever get better?"

I shake my head. "I kind of learned that if I just push it away, you know, don't think about it, that I can keep going. I got very good at not feeling it anymore. It didn't stop hurting, I just sort of stopped letting myself remember to hurt."

Kyle holds out his hand and I take it. He is warm under my fingertips, warm and strong and alive.

"That day at school, when you smiled at me and said hello, it was like, I don't know how to explain it. It was like, I'd been in this really dark place. It was so hard just to get out of bed because, I didn't feel him around anymore. I was just really lonely I think. And then, just when I was sure I wouldn't be able to do it, there you were. I mean, that day I was planning on leaving the team. I just didn't think I could face it. And there you were, like this light in the middle of all of the darkness. And it felt like Logan was there, like he knew I needed you so he sent you to me."

He shakes his head like he feels stupid saying the words. I squeeze his hand.

"I believe that too. Logan wants us to have each other. I know it. I can feel it. Because as much as it hurts sometimes, it hurts less when I'm with you."

"Zoe," Logan's voice is tight.

I can't look at him, I won't look at him. Because if I do, I'll cry. I'll cry because I understand now why he stopped seeing me. He wasn't leaving me at all, he was letting me go. And that has to be harder than anything else.

"Zoe, it's here."

Those words are enough to make my head jerk up, and sure enough, at the end of the bar The Reaper is standing there staring at me.

I stiffen, not sure what to do. It isn't moving and I know no one else can see it. But if I go to the bathroom again Kyle will think I have a medical problem. And I can't ask to leave before the expensive meal even comes. But, what if Logan is right and it does try something, right here. My god, what if I choke on my pasta and die?

I glance over at Kyle, who is still clutching my hand.

It would kill him, I realize. He thinks I'm some kind of miracle, a sign from the universe that everything is going to be okay.

But I'm not. I'm just a horrible person who used him to get close to the others to get the dirt on Kaylee. I swallow the bitter guilt.

"I got this," Logan says as the waiter approaches with a massive tray of food balanced on one hand.

Closing his eyes I hear him whisper my name before reaching out and slapping the tray, sending the food flying into the air. It lands, covering both Kyle and I with bits of pasta and fish and veggies.

The waiter is mortified. The entire restaurant stares, some people laughing, some clapping. A bunch of the staff rush over with towels. The manager follows quickly, offering not only his deepest apologies, but a free meal.

I just laugh. Kyle laughs with me.

"Its fine," I offer the poor, distraught waiter who doused me in Alfredo sauce. "Really, I'll live."

Kyle seems fine, relieved that I'm not angry or causing any more of a scene. He calmly accepts the meal vouchers and we hurry to his truck, still picking pieces of food out of our hair and belly laughing. He opens my door, pulling a long noodle off the back of my sweater.

"I'm so sorry," he offers with a wide smile.

I shrug. "No big deal. You aren't the one who dumped a tray of food on me. And besides," I pick a chunk of salmon off the top of his head, "you got it just as bad as I did."

"So, does this mean the date's over?"

I bite my bottom lip, an idea hitting me out of

nowhere. "It doesn't have to be."

"Zoe," Logan warns, his voice stern.

"I have an idea. It's a little stupid, very risky, and mildly illegal. What do you think?" I ask, my hands resting on his chest.

"I think I'm in."

I climb in the truck, whispering to Logan as Kyle rounds the cab to the other side.

"Logan, go back to my house. Keep an eye on my mom."

"What are you going to do?" he demands, but Kyle is already in the truck. With a huff Logan vanishes, leaving me alone in the dark truck with my poor, fish covered boyfriend. He puts the key in and revs the engine.

"Where to?"

"You know how to get to the caverns?"

He nods and we speed off. The caverns are a pretty popular tourist spot on the outskirts of town. And they are full of the one thing my hooded friend can't handle. Iron.

Twenty

THE PARKING LOT IS LOCKED, no surprise there. The caverns are closed in early September for the year, mostly because they are so far underground that the temperatures barely get above freezing in the heat of summer. Once the weather cools, the caves become a frozen tomb for anyone stupid enough to venture in. Kyle follows me as we hike around back, picking up a barely noticeable trail from the rear of the main building. The Parks Department built a shop and tour headquarters right over the entrance to the caverns, making it impossible to get in when the building itself is closed.

Unless you know the back entrance.

Its pitch black and only the light from my phone illuminates the path. Still, Kyle follows me without question or hesitation. At one point, I look up, trying to get my bearings. Then I see it. A small hill juts out into the middle of a clearing. It looks like it's a giant rock in the hillside, but I know better. As Kyle follows me I turn, pointing to the south face and the tight crack splitting the rock in two.

"There. That's the way in."

Squeezing through the crack I find myself in a hollow stone chamber. The walls are damp inside, and the sound of trickling water is far off, but echoes around us. Once Kyle is inside I grab the old lantern I'd left there after my last visit, still right where I'd tucked it away, and I bring it to beautiful light.

"Whoa," he says, looking at the walls around us.

"Most of the caves in this area are limestone, but you see the red streaks down the walls? That's iron."

"It looks like paintings in the stone."

The patterns are amazing, but that's not the only reason I brought him here. The air in the cavern is cold, easily ten degrees colder than outside. I jerk my head for him to follow me down the narrow tunnel and around the corner. When we spill out into the next chamber, it's raining inside. Well, not raining exactly.

"See that?" I point to a pool of water only a few feet in front of us.

"It's a natural spring. A hot spring actually."

"What's that smell?"

"Sulfur. From the water. But it's not bad."

Reaching down I stick my hand in the water. It's not hot, but compared to the cold air, it feels like bath tub temperature.

"The moisture in the air is from this."

Kneeling beside me Kyle sticks his hand in. He

looks over at me, grinning.

"So, you wanna go for a soak?" I ask boldly.

"Hell yeah."

"Cool, you turn around while I get in."

He grins, puts his hand over his eyes and turns his back to me. I slip down to my bra and panties and slide into the warm water.

"Okay, your turn."

He turns back to me, wide grin still firmly in place. He strips down to his boxers and climbs in beside me.

"This is amazing Zoe."

"I know, right?"

I keep waiting for the fact that I'm half naked in a pool with a guy I hardly know to register as a huge mistake in my brain, but it doesn't happen. We just laugh and talk and everything feels so...relaxed. It's almost a shame when he finally sighs.

"As fun as this is, I think we should be getting home. It's after midnight."

He's right. But I have a trunk load of problems waiting for me at home, and I'd give just about anything to not have to deal with them for just a few more hours.

I slip back into the water so only my face is above the surface and stare at the stone above me. How has my life gotten so complicated? What did I do to deserve this particular bag of insanity?

I don't hear Kyle make his way through the water to me, I just feel his arms wrap around me and the next thing I know, I'm pressed tightly against him as he lifts me out of the pool, kissing me as we move. When my feet hit stone, I'm still tangled in his arms, my hands running along the lines of his body of their own accord. He strokes my hair, my back. Slowly, like an ember being brought to flame, I feel the heat rise inside me. Even the tiny, wet scraps of clothes between us seem like too much. I feel him stiffen, pulling away just a little. Some deep, primal part of my brain wants to end the painful separation. But then there's a soft voice in the back of my head. The voice of reason.

And it sounds a lot like Logan.

I force myself to step back, not really releasing him, but getting a hint of breathing room between us. I lock on to Kyle's eyes. His expression is wild, flushed. He's panting almost as hard as I am.

"Best. First. Date. Ever," He says, kissing me quickly one more time before releasing me and scooping up his clothes, and turning away.

"I'm going to go get dressed. Over here," he says breathlessly, not turning back to look at me.

The drive home is quiet. Not in an awkward way, but in a blissful, calm way. Maybe I'm just tired, but I scoot to the middle seat of the truck, leaning against him as he drives. He slips an arm around me and I close my eyes, just for a minute.

Or at least if feels like it's only a minute. The next time I open them we are pulling into my driveway. My hair is still damp and there's a wet spot on Kyle's shirt where I'd been resting. I let him walk me to my door, kissing him goodnight on my porch step. He drives off and I step inside, faced immediately with a sour faced Logan.

"What?" I whisper, knowing mom is probably fast asleep in her room.

"I was worried sick. Do you know what time it is?"

I burst out with a laugh and walk to my room. "I didn't realize you were the curfew police."

"I tried to find you, Zoe. I closed my eyes like I always do, thought of you, and there was nothing. It was like you'd just vanished off the face of the earth or…"

I stop mid step, looking back over my shoulder at him. I jerk my head, motioning for him to come into my room then shut the door.

"You thought I was dead."

He rakes his fingers through his hair. "I didn't know what to think. You were gone and Bruno was gone."

"He likes to be called Kyle."

"I don't care if he likes to dress up in women's underwear and be called Nancy. I couldn't find you!"

He raises his hands in the air, making a gesture like he wants to choke me. Then he throws them in the air and stomps off.

"You almost gave me a heart attack, Zoe. Seriously. If I wasn't already dead, I could have died."

I snicker again.

"Relax, Logan. I took Kyle someplace safe. Where neither you nor The Reaper could find us."

"Where?"

"None of your business, Casper the Stalky Ghost."

"Fine. Whatever. I'm just glad you're okay. Wait. Why is your hair wet?"

I pull at the damp, wavy strands around my face. "Oh, yeah. I should probably go shower. Somebody dumped a tray of food on me."

"Hey, it got you out of there, didn't it?"

I nod, grabbing a towel and my jammies. "Yes, clever plan Logan. Next time maybe you can light me on fire or something."

"Hey," he reaches out, grabbing my arm. This time I feel it, his cool skin on mine.

"Yeah?"

"I'm glad you're alright. And I'm sorry about before. If you want me around, I'm here. For however long we have."

I swallow. Probably not the best time to admit I'd nearly jumped Kyle's bones at the cavern. I don't know what to say so I just nod and head for the shower.

The hot water only makes me feel worse. I can still feel Kyle pressed against me, I can taste him on my tongue. Slowly I wash the bubbles out of my hair.

If there was any kind of justice that stupid Reaper would take me and leave them both alone. If the world worked the way it was supposed to, it would have been me that died, not Logan. Not my dad.

I straighten up. Maybe that's why it's here. Maybe it really should have been me. Maybe this time, the universe will get it right.

I let myself sleep in longer than I mean to the next day. But I'm bone tired and I don't have any plans, so I figure why not? Other than answering an early morning text from Kyle who is off to a full day of lacrosse practice, I don't even move until almost noon.

The knock at my door makes me jump.

Carlos peeks his head inside. "You decent, Zoe Bowie?"

"As decent as I ever am. Come on in."

Carlos walks in, shutting the door behind him. "Um, is he here?"

Logan waves from his spot in my chair.

I point in his direction.

"Hey, Logan," Carlos offers cheerfully.

Logan waves, not looking back from the movie he's watching.

"He says hey."

"Cool. So, I had my date with Mr. Perfect last night," Carlos begins with no preamble.

I sit up, swinging my legs over the side of my bed. "Great, how did it go?"

"It was a little weird at first, but it turns out he's a huge boxing fan, so he and my dad totally hit it off. It was per-fect. And," he takes a deep breath, "I asked him to Homecoming."

"And he said yes?"

"No, he said no. I mean, it's sort of weird for a college guy to be dating a high school senior, but he asked me to go to his Homecoming instead, so I said yes. It was—"

"Perfect," Logan and I answer in unison.

"Exactly. So, what are we doing today?" he asks, walking over to my closet and rummaging through the hangers.

"I was actually thinking some research might be in order," I offer, walking over to Logan who looks up at me curiously. "Maybe we can't figure out who killed you. But maybe we can at least figure out what that Reaper thing is and what it wants."

Logan sits forward, his hands on his knees. "That's worth a shot. Maybe we can figure out how to get rid of it."

"That's what I was thinking too," I say. But it's a lie. Mostly, I want to know what it is, and what it wants. Because, if it really is after me, no way in hell am I going to let anyone else I love get hurt or killed in my place. If it's really here for me, then I'm going to go with it, I've already decided.

Logan gives me a doubtful look, but Carlos just tosses me an armful of clothes.

"Here. Go get ready. We can go to the library, and grab something to eat on the way."

Saluting him I dash off to the bathroom and change. When I get back Carlos is talking to himself. Or to Logan, probably.

"What are you two talking about?"

Carlos hands me my messenger bag. "What? Nothing. Let's go."

I glance over at Logan who puts his hands in the air like he has no idea what I'm talking about. Fine. Whatever.

I follow Carlos through the house and as I pass the kitchen I notice a huge bundle of flowers on the table.

"Oh. Those came this morning," Logan says, his voice dry and unimpressed. "Your mom brought them in before she left.

I veer into the kitchen and pull the tag out of the flowers.

Thanks for the best first date ever.

Love, Kyle

I stick the card in the back pocket of my jeans before Carlos can see it and start asking embarrassing questions I don't want to answer. I turn and Logan is literally looking over my shoulder, one eyebrow raised.

I roll my eyes and step through him, following Carlos out to his car.

As soon as we open the door I see it. Across the street, standing in the stark daylight, it's brown robe billowing gently. Logan sees it too, stepping in front of me.

"Get in the car," he orders. "Head to the library. I'll meet you there."

"What are you going to do?"

He shakes his head, "I'm going to try to get some answers."

"You coming, Zoe?" Carlos asks from his car.

I grab Logan's arm, solid only for a moment. "Be careful."

He leans back, kissing me quickly on the cheek. "I'm always careful."

I sigh, climbing into the car. "Says the dead guy."

Twenty-One

THE LIBRARY IS FILLED with screaming toddlers. Kids story time, I remember as I wade through the horde of midgets. My dad used to bring me when I was little. Luckily, the study area is off to the back, far beyond the kids section and down the stairs. Taking the first left into the bowels of the library we head for the computers, and take seats opposite each other. Logan appears before I can even launch the internet.

"He vanished before I could get any answers out of him."

I nod, not wanting to freak out Carlos, and begin my search. An hour later and all I have to show for it is a stiff neck, blood shot eyes, and the beginnings of a nasty headache.

"Does it have wings?" Carlos asks across the table.

He's staring at the computer so hard it looks like he's trying to figure out how to climb inside the monitor.

"No," I answer.

"What about a scythe?"

"Nope."

He frowns, clicking the mouse. "What about a trident?"

I raise an eyebrow, "Really."

He nods.

"No, no trident. What are you looking at?"

"Online catalogue of death figures," he says as if it should be obvious.

Because, duh, I totally should have expected that.

"Okay, no…no. No…"

"You're talking to yourself Carlos."

He shushes me.

"Here, how about this? The Mintle. It comes from ancient Samaria, a sort of death omen. It says they appear with a white or brown robe, and they don't cause death so much as witness it. The ancient Samarians believed the Mintle was responsible for leading the dead to the afterlife. There's even a picture. Sort of."

I get out of my chair and round the desk, looking over his shoulder. Picture is a deceptive word. A crudely drawn sketch would be more accurate. Basically, it looks like any generic person in a long hooded cape.

"Maybe. Any other references?"

He shakes his head. "None that fit. But there's a footnote with a reference. A book from the late 60's."

"Great. Give me the number and I'll see if it's in the catalogue here. If we get lucky, they might have a copy."

Going back over to the main catalogue computer

I type in the numbers as he calls them out. Zero in stock. Of course. So I decide to try a general sweep and type in Mintle as a subject and keyword. One hit. But there's no shelf number.

"Crap. I'm gonna go see if the librarian knows where this book is. I'll be right back. But keep digging, just in case this isn't what we're looking for."

He salutes and returns to typing and I head for the Information Desk where a slender brunette is talking on the phone. She hangs up.

"Can I help you?"

I hand over the slip of paper I've written the title on. "Yeah, I found this in the catalogue, but there's no shelf number."

She types it onto her computer, lowering her glasses from her head onto her eyes.

"Let's see. Okay, well this is in the archives. It's not on the shelf."

I frown. "Oh, well, how does one go about getting a book out of the archives?"

She stares at me like I must be joking.

"It's important. History assignment."

She huffs, looking completely put out. "The archived books are all in the sub-basement."

She points to the stairs. "Look for the shelf labeled reference. The boxes will be in alphabetical order by author."

Nice, way to send me to a rat infested basement on my own you crappy excuse for a librarian. The phone lights up, indicating a call. She hands me back the paper and quickly answers it.

Stuffing the paper in my back pocket I head for the elevator at the far end of the room. I tap Carlos on the shoulder as I walk by.

"Hey, I have to go play Where's Waldo for this stupid book. If I'm not back in five, send in the National Guard."

"Can do."

The sub-basement is brighter than I expected. Rows of overhead lights flicker on as soon as I step off the elevator. Of course it stinks like stale cigarettes and old books. It's a large, concrete room with rows of grey metal shelves and white boxes. At the front of each row is a small sign. Fiction, Non Fiction, Audio, and Reference. Making a bee line down the reference aisle I start scanning for books, looking for the S shelf. Saunders is the author's last name.

The lights overhead buzz with electricity and somewhere I hear the tell-tale squeaks of a mouse. Or with my luck, an army of mice. With rabies. And knives. Yep, rabid, ninja mice. That would be my luck. I finally find the S boxes. A whole freaking shelf of them. I decide to start at the top and work my way down. Grabbing the first box off the shelf I let it fall to my feet and pull the lid off. A moth flies out and I let out a nervous shriek.

"Hey, let's go down to the creepy ass basement. That sounds like a great plan," I mutter to myself feeling like a complete wuss.

Worst. Plan. Ever.

It takes me all of three seconds to realize this isn't the right box and return it to the shelf. Grabbing the next box I repeat the process. Finally, three boxes later, I hit the jackpot. Pulling the ancient, tattered book out of the box I fold myself cross legged onto the cold floor and open the book up in my lap. The pages are musty and faded, even the glue binding the spine is failing, and loose pages out of order are stuffed haphazardly inside the cloth cover.

I examine the pages carefully, looking for any mention of the Mintle. Finally, I see it.

"The Mintle…blah, blah, blah, death spirit. Blah, blah, blah. Usually depicted as a female with hollow eye sockets and skeletal features. Ugh. Can rotate head completely around. Eeew. That's just unnecessary. And… always accompanied by a large black dog. Sorry Mintle, you aren't my ring wraith." I slam the book closed with a dusty puff and return it to the box.

I'm making my way back to the elevator when I feel it. A chill air blows past me like someone's switched on an air conditioner. I turn slowly, praying that it's just Logan, even though I know it isn't. Logan, despite being very, very dead, still somehow smells like rain and water. I don't smell that now.

I just smell musty books and death.

It's at the far end of the stacks, hovering there silently. If not for the subtle movement of its robe, I would think it was just some ass-hat in a costume playing a prank. But its feet aren't touching the ground.

I don't scream. I just sort of tense up, my muscles locking in terror as it watches me from under its large hood. Its face is shrouded in shadows, and part of me is really glad. I have the distinct feeling this is not a creature I want to be eye to eye with.

Slowly, as if carried by a breeze, it floats toward me. I straighten my back, my feet firmly planted. I'm not going to run. It doesn't even feel like an option. Whatever this thing wants from me, I just want it over with. Lowering my chin I ball my hands into fists. I doubt that beating this thing violently about the head will do any good, but hey, what's the harm in trying?

It gets to within three feet of me and stops, its hands folded into its sleeves.

"What are you waiting for, a freaking invitation? Come on!"

I stand there, my jaw clenched so tight I can feel the ache in my teeth, challenging the spirit. It doesn't move.

"I'm right here. I'm not going anywhere. So tell me what you want or get lost."

A deep rattling breath fills its robes, words escaping from under the hood with a sour hiss.

"You. It's you."

"What's me?" I demand.

"It's you. It's you." The voice keeps repeating, growing louder and steadier each time it repeats. "It's you. It's you. It's you."

Soon the voice is deep and echoing inside my head like a bell. I drop to my knees, pressing my hands to my ears to try to block out the sound, but I can't. It's coming from inside me, resonating through my body and bouncing around inside my skull. The voice is like a vice in my head, squeezing my brain. Pain shoots through my skull like shards of glass, shattering inside me.

I squeeze my eyes closed. "Stop it. Please stop." The pain is unbearable, blinding. It's like I'm going to explode. "Please. Logan help me."

And just like that the voice is gone. I'm shaking, my heart pounding. My head aches and I feel a trickle of something wet roll down the side of my neck. I touch my fingers to it and they come away bloody. Pitching forward on my knees I press my head against the cold, cement floor and just breathe. Logan appears beside me in the blink of an eye.

"Zoe, I heard you call out for me is everything—" He stops, dropping to his knees beside me. "Zoe, what happened?"

I don't know what to say, or if I could even form words. My throat is raw, the pain still ebbing from my body. I look over at him. His eyes are wild, desperate. He's trying to touch me but he can't make himself solid enough.

"I'm fine," I manage weakly.

But there's something in his expression, something broken and defeated and afraid. I think Logan is realizing, maybe for the first time, that he can't protect me. And I think it's killing him.

Using the shelf for support, I climb to my feet, wiping the blood away with the sleeve of my shirt. My knees are still weak, but I manage to make my way to the elevator with Logan beside me the whole way.

"What happened?" he's asking. "Did it attack you?"

I take a deep breath and hit the up button.

"Yeah. Sort of. I don't think it meant to hurt me. It was trying to tell me something."

"Trying to tell you what?"

The doors slide open and I step inside, resting my head against the wall.

"That somehow, all of this is my fault. Logan, I think that somehow, it's my fault you died."

Twenty-Two

I GATHER CARLOS AND MY STUFF and head home for a long, hot shower. I fill them both in on the full details during the ride back to my house. They are both too worried to leave my side, even when I tell them I'm fine and just really need a shower and a nap.

The hot water pounds on my back, relaxing away the tension as I stand in the shower, rinsing the sweet smelling soap off my skin. When I step out, wrapping my towel around me I freeze. In the mirror fog someone has written my name over and over. And I know it wasn't Logan. I shiver, even though the room is hot and my skin is nearly burnt pink, wiping away the message with my hand.

I comb my fingers through my wet hair, tugging out any tangles. I stare at myself for a minute. No way am I going to let some stupid wanna be Reaper get the best of me. I refuse to be afraid. I refuse to let the people I love be afraid for me.

After drying off I step into a fresh set of clothes,

this time black leggings and a long dress shirt with green lace and a thick belt. Taking my time I blow dry my hair, apply a layer of lotion to my face, and just a little bit of lip gloss. By the time I'm done I look like I'm ready for a night out instead of looking like I've just been attacked by a freaking ghost. I toss the hairbrush in the sink and walk back to my room where my boys are waiting for me. Logan is stretched out across my bed and Carlos is sitting in the chair flipping through channels on TV.

"You look better," Logan says calmly.

"I feel better," I admit. Nothing like having your brain nearly squeezed like a grape to put things in perspective.

Carlos spins around in the chair, holding out a stack of papers for me.

"Here's everything I found on Death Spirits, Reapers, and haunting. I didn't see anything that looked quite like what you described, but who knows? Something might jump out at you."

I take the papers, forcing a smile.

"Thanks."

"Are you sure you're alright?" He asks, his face twisted with concern.

"Fine."

"So totally not fine then."

I shrug. "Pretty much. But I'll survive."

"For now," Logan cuts in. He has his hands tucked behind his head and he's glaring at me.

"I told you, Logan, it wasn't attacking me, not on

purpose anyway."

He sits up, "Exactly. Imagine what it could have done if it was *trying* to hurt you."

"Well, what exactly would you like me to do about it, Logan? I can't carry an iron pipe around with me all the time. Short of figuring out what it is and how to ship it back to wherever it came from, how should I be spending my time?"

My voice is sharp, crueler than I mean for it to be and he flinches.

"Well, how about you start by not wandering off alone to deserted basements? I thought you were smarter than that."

"Excuse me, but I was trying to figure this mess out. I mean, for shit's sake, I'm here, doing all the work, trying to help you fix your screwed up afterlife, and all you do is mess with my head and drive me insane. You wanna talk to me about being stupid, you couldn't even die right."

Carlos stands up, holding up his hands. "Okay, I'm only getting half this convo, but Zoe, your bitch meter is hitting a twelve. I need you at a six, okay? And Logan, whatever buttons you're pushing, you'd better back off before she goes nuclear."

Logan glares at him.

"She started it."

I snort. "He can't hear you, polterdouche."

"Zoe," Carlos almost growls my name. "Knock it off. We are all on the same team here, okay."

"Yeah, listen to your friend."

I lunge for Logan, who skitters off the bed like he's actually afraid I might try to pummel him. Carlos grabs my arm.

"Look, I have to get going. I'm supposed to be helping my mom set up for dad's surprise birthday party tonight. Can you two get along or should I hose you down before I go?"

I huff and pull my arm away.

"We will be just fine."

Kissing my forehead Carlos whispers.

"Zoe, play nice. And call me if you need anything."

I nod, folding my arms across my chest.

As soon as he's gone Logan starts in again.

"You know, you're like a lollypop triple dipped in crazy."

"Somewhere, the magical kingdom of Douche-Bagistan has lost its king. Because here you are."

He chuckles. "Okay, that was a good one."

I flop down in my chair, kicking my legs over the arm. "Thanks."

"What now?" he asks after a minute of silence.

I hold up the papers. "I have homework. And you should probably go back to retracing your steps from the night you died. We are literally out of leads now. Your memory might be our only shot at getting you back where you belong."

Logan sits near my feet, resting against the end of my bed. "Zoe, what happens if I go, and that thing is still here?"

I look up at him, not sure what to say.

He runs his fingers through his hair, looking away. "I'm just saying that maybe we shouldn't be so focused on my moving on. Not right now. Not when you're in danger."

A long, jagged spike of fear stabs into my chest. I clutch the bottle cap necklace still dangling from my neck.

"The thing is, whatever The Reaper wants, whatever it's here for, it's on me. Maybe it's fate. If so… I'm not going to fight it Logan. If it's my time, then it's my time. Maybe it should have been me all along. Maybe that's what it's trying to tell me."

He shakes his head. "You can't really believe that?"

I shrug. "Maybe I do. Maybe I'm just tired of trying to keep moving, keep living every day like I'm not already half dead inside."

"Zoe—"

I hold up my hand.

"Let me just say this. If it's my time or not, whatever happens, I want to help you first. I want to know that you are in a better place, that you aren't trapped here. Because if something did happen to me, you'd be all alone, and I couldn't bear that."

"And I can't bear the thought of losing you."

I bite my bottom lip, looking away. "I know."

"No, you don't. I look at you, and you say you're half dead inside, but all I see is this fire all around you, this burning passion—this *life*. It's like you're a sun in the sky, when everything else is darkness. I feel you. And when we touch, it's like a little bit of that life is rubbing off on me. So you can say you're tired and you can say you're going to accept your fate, but believe me when I tell you that you're too strong for that. You have too much fight in you to just let go. So, don't let go, okay? Promise me you'll keep fighting."

I smile weakly. "I promise."

We spend the next few hours going over the printouts while Logan keeps watch from my window. I catch myself staring at him from time to time, thinking about his words and the promise I'm not sure I can keep.

My phone vibrates on my dresser and I get up to check it.

"Who is it?" Logan asks.

I frown. "It's Kyle. He wants me to meet him. He says…Logan, he says he needs to see me right now. That he found out something about the person who killed you."

I look up, my eyes locking on to Logan's. It could be the break we've been waiting for, but something feels off. Deep in my gut, something is wrong and I can't put my finger on what it is.

"He wants to meet me at The Tower."

Logan strides up beside me, reading the text over my shoulder.

"Why The Tower?" he asks.

I shake my head. "No clue. Unless…Logan. What if he found something? Or what if Becker said something? Whatever it is, we need to know."

"Try calling. Maybe he will just talk to you over the phone."

It's a good idea so I dial him up. It goes straight to voice mail.

"No dice, Frodo. I'm gonna have to go meet him."

"I'm coming too."

I nod. Of course he is. Let's just hope things don't get quite as intense as the last time Kyle and I were alone together.

"And Zoe," he pauses pointing to my bed, "Take the poker."

I grab the iron poker and my messenger bag and head for the car.

Twenty-Three

I T'S DUSK BY THE TIME I pull into the gravel parking area beside the radio tower. The last glowing rays of sunshine are burning orange and red in the sky. There's no sign of Kyle's truck so I shoot him a quick text which he returns immediately.

"I'm on my way."

The gravel crunches under my boots as I walk through the dense woods to The Tower. The police have taped off the bridge and the base of the tower itself. Without hesitation I rip it away, climbing to the top to get a better view of the sunset across the river.

"It's really beautiful," Logan whispers in my ear.

"Yeah, it is."

There are so many things I want to say to Logan in that moment, as I watch the sun disappear behind the horizon. But it all seems so empty. What could I say that I haven't already said? What can I tell him that he doesn't already know? The truth is, I'm ripping myself to shreds. Part of me is dying to be with him, part of me is aching to set him free. It's like being lost and not knowing which way will take you home.

I check the time on my phone. It's been almost forty minutes now. What is taking Kyle so long? I shiver, wishing I'd thought to grab my jacket. I text him but he doesn't respond. The uneasy churning in my stomach grows.

"Logan, will you go check on Kyle for me? See what's taking him so long?"

He nods. "Sure. Stay here. I'll be right back."

Yeah, just in case I get the homicidal need to run off into the dark, cold woods alone. I salute him and he vanishes. I switch my phone to flashlight mode and take a seat on the cold diamond steel floor.

A few minutes pass before I hear the tell-tale sound of tires on gravel. Climbing down carefully I decide to meet him at the parking area and retrieve the spare jacket I know he keeps in his truck. I walk through the brush, surprised to see the person standing in front of me.

"Mr. Mason?" I ask, shining the phone light in his face.

"Zoe, what are you doing here?" he asks, confused.

I point behind me. "I was just meeting up with someone. What are you doing here?"

He holds up a bunch of roses. "I come up here sometimes to think. Where's your friend?"

I open my mouth to tell him that Kyle isn't here yet when I realize what's behind him. A brand new black

Honda with a silver medal dangling from the rear view mirror. The blood turns to ice in my veins. Of course, as the team coach, he'd have gotten a medal too. The puzzle pieces start clicking together in my brain. Kaylee's mystery man, the one who 'doesn't go to our school'. If Logan found out about them, he would lose his job. His family. He has a wife and a little baby for Christsake.

Baby.

Oh my god, he was the father of Kaylee's baby. He must have freaked out when she told him and he killed her.

"Yeah, um. Kyle is just down the road. He should be here any second so…"

"Is that so?" he asks casually.

I nod. "Yeah, I'm just getting a sweater out of my car. It's getting cold. But I can leave you to your… whatever."

I try to slip past him to my car, but he grabs my arm.

"Bruno isn't coming, Zoe. I'm sorry to break it to you. But no one is coming."

I swallow. That isn't exactly true. He holds up Kyle's cell phone. I recognize the case, it's got the superman logo on it. "He misplaced this today at practice. But don't worry. The police will find it, here with you."

It only takes me a second to process what he's saying. He's going to kill me and let Kyle take the fall for it. And if they think he did this to me, they will find some way to pin Kaylee's murder on him too. Pushing me against the back of my car he releases my arm and goes for my throat, his big, sweaty hands choking me. Rearing up I kick him in the nuts, hard. He loosens his grip just enough for me to break his hold and roll to the side. Getting my feet under me quickly I run off into the darkness.

"Logan," I scream as I run to the tower.

He appears in a flash.

"Zoe, Bruno is at home doing a report on the computer he's not—" I trip, landing at his feet.

"Yeah, I got the memo."

Mr. Mason bursts through the trees, flashlight in hand.

"Come on, Zoe. Let's not make this hard."

"Yeah, right," I scream, picking up a large tree branch and holding it like a baseball bat.

"Zoe, I have an idea, you need to get him talking, okay? I'll be right back."

I barely have time to breathe before he's gone again.

"Damn it, Logan!"

Mr. Mason freezes, tilting his head to the side.

"You really see him don't you?"

I lower my chin, "What do you know about it?"

He nods, "I heard you talking to yourself after class. It didn't take me long to realize who you were talking to. I didn't believe it at first, but I saw you with Bruno and the others—a group you've never had any interest in before—and I thought to myself, why would a smart girl like Zoe join that crowd. So I started watching you, watching them. You put on a good show, but I could see it. The vague detachment. You were trying to figure out what happened."

"How could you do it? Logan trusted you. And Kaylee…" I trail off. I was going to say that she loved him, but I'm not actually sure that's true. So I settle for the next best thing. "She was carrying your baby."

He laughs out loud. "Yes, what a wonderful surprise that would have been for my wife. Not to mention the fact that I'd be out of a job—forever. No school would ever hire me with a scandal like that on my record."

I snort, "Wow, you are like, king of the douche fairies, you know that?"

"Put the branch down and let's talk about this."

I swing the stick just a little, "Oh, I'm sorry do I have 'stupid' tattooed to my forehead? You've already killed two people. You really think I'm going to be number three? Guess again."

Logan reappears beside me. I glance over.

"And where did you run off to?"

"Relax, I called in the cavalry."

I laugh dryly. "You wanna explain that one to me, because seriously."

"You're talking to him right now, aren't you?" Mr. Mason asks, his face amused.

"Yeah. He says being dead is great, you should try it. Maybe just go," I jerk my head back, "jump off a cliff or something. I won't try to stop you."

"Oh," he smiles, "I don't think so."

Logan walks over to Mr. Mason, circling him slowly.

"I remember now. I remember him begging me not to say anything. Kaylee even tried to plead his case. I told him he was a pervert and that I was going straight to the police. When I turned around to leave, he hit me in the back of the head with something. Then he grabbed me by the shirt and dragged me onto the bridge."

"You hit him in the back of the head and dragged him to the bridge. You threw him over, and let the rocks and the water do the rest," I repeat and Mr. Mason pales. "What, you weren't really sure were you? Until right now you thought I might just be some crazy girl seeing things that aren't there. But guess what? You're only half right."

I throw the branch at him, nailing him in the side of the head, and run. Ducking into the trees I sprint through the woods. It's dark, too dark to see anything and I must have dropped my phone back at the car. I trip over a branch, flying forward to my feet. Logan is there in an instant.

"Follow me," he says offering me a hand up. I grab it and he's solid, as solid as he's ever been. I let him lead me through the forest, off a narrow path into a bunch of tall ferns.

"Here, Zoe. My phone is there," he points to a large hollow tree. Taking a deep breath I lunge for it. Grabbing the device I hold down the power button, waiting for it to turn on.

"Come on you stupid thing, come on."

I hear Mr. Mason scrambling through the brush behind me just as the screen flickers to life. I have a split second to hit 911 and send, throwing the phone as far as I can in the darkness before I feel his hand tangle into my hair, yanking me to my feet. He warps the other arm around me and I'm stuck. I kick and scream, but I'm no match for his strength.

Logan lunges for him, but only manages to move right through us, falling to the ground. Mr. Mason drags me away, kicking and thrashing. I manage to get loose once, but he has me again, this time with both arms squeezing across my chest so tightly I can't scream, I can't even breathe. Black spots form in my sight, driving away the little bit of light the moon is providing. He half drags half carries me back to the tower, tossing me to the ground at his feet. Climbing on top of me in a way that's violently intimate he stuffs my arms under his knees and leans down hard, pressing all his weight down on me.

"You really are a pretty girl, Zoe. It's a shame I couldn't add you to my collection. We could have had a lot of fun you and me." He runs his hand down the side of my face and I bite at it. Drawing back he punches me in the face. Pain explodes like dynamite. It feels like every bone in my cheek shatters on impact, my teeth crashing together, blood instantly pooling in my mouth, threatening to drown me. I spit it up in his face.

He draws back to hit me again and I feel his

weight lifting off me. The relief is swift, cold air flooding my lungs. I roll to my side, coughing and spitting out blood onto the dark grass. Glancing over I see The Reaper. It's hovering there in the moonlight, staring at me. Looking over my shoulder I see my rescuer. Kyle and Mr. Mason are grappling over by the bridge.

Logan drops to his knees beside me.

"Told you I called the cavalry."

I shake my head slowly, "How?"

"I will explain later, right now you need to get out of here."

I struggle to my feet. Mr. Mason has Kyle in a headlock. Grabbing the branch off the ground as I go, I run toward them, swinging the branch and nailing Mr. Mason in the side of the head with a very satisfying crack. He falls to the side and Kyle gasps for air. I wrap my arms around him, trying to help him up. But Mr. Mason is quick to recover, his face covered with blood as he grabs me, spins me to face him, and pushes me backward. I miss the bridge by inches, reaching out and grabbing the old cable before I tumble helplessly off the side. The last thing I see is Kyle bum rushing him, head down, and spearing him in the gut. I slip, my feet scrambling to find some kind of foot hold in the dirt of the cliff face. My arm is on fire, clutching with one hand to the cable of the bridge. I look up and see The Reaper leaning over, looking down at me. It reaches over, holding one stark white hand out to me. I struggle, screaming for help.

Then it hits me.

Help isn't coming. Even if the police got my 911, they are still fifteen minutes away, and that's if the call even went through. This is it. I'm going to hang here while Mr. Mason kills Kyle, then comes for me. I'll die, and Logan will be stuck here.

With a desperate push of energy I pull myself up far enough to grab the cable with my other hand, and even with the burning in my arm, I somehow get my stomach on the bridge, then one knee, then the other.

Pushing through the yellow tape I rush at Mr. Mason, knocking him to the ground. One sharp punch to the throat and he's gasping. He swings at my face and I see too late that he has a rock in his hand. It connects with my temple, completely cutting off my vision to that eye. But I don't fall. Another punch to the neck, this time I hear bone crack and he gasps, wheezing for air. He drops the rock and I pick it up, smashing it into the side of his face over and over.

I'm not sure if it's instinct, or rage, or the fear that he might keep getting up and keep coming after me, but I keep swinging until his face is so covered in blood that it doesn't even look like a face anymore.

"Zoe," Kyle coughs, rubbing his neck from where he sways on hands and knees.

"Zoe, you can stop now," Logan says gently. I look over my shoulder, through my one good eye at The Reaper. I expect it to come for me, or Mr. Mason, or Logan, but it just vanishes.

"Huh. Looks like it wasn't my time to go after all,"

I whisper and fall, rolling off of Mr. Mason and onto my back. I blink once up at the bright white moon before everything goes dark.

Twenty-Four

A S IT TURNS OUT, dying feels a lot like falling asleep. There's no pain or fear, just a quiet, accepting calm. Or at least that's how I remember it.

Living, however, hurts like a son of a bitch. I scratch at the hollow of my arm, where the IV is poking out of my skin. The tape itches like crazy, and that's actually the least of my problems. The vision comes back in my right eye after a few days. Or maybe weeks. Who the hell knows? I'm on so many painkillers there's no way to really know how much time is passing. Kyle comes in and sits with me sometimes. He's pretty bruised up himself and I have to be careful not to make him laugh beacuse he can't breathe on account of his broken ribs. He reads to me or shows me funny internet videos on his new phone.

Logan never leaves. He's always there, in the corner of the room, watching me. I feel bad for him. I really thought that once he had his memory back, he'd be able to move on. Maybe that isn't it at all. Maybe it never was. I try not to bring it up. Not even when he crawls in bed beside me at night.

The police have been in and out. Mr. Mason is still in a coma, or so they tell me. Part of me hopes he dies, part of me hopes he lives to answer for what he did. Either way, I won't be butt hurt about it. Mom is in and out all the time, working at the hospital has its perks. She gets to see me on every break. She doesn't make me talk about what happened, though she was there when I had to tell the cops how it went down. I leave out the part about Logan, of course. I'd like to see the outside of a hospital at some point in my life. The twins come by with flowers, Becker and Cassidy bring magazines. Even Madison and Becca come by, though I suspect only to get the gossip on what happened.

Today, Carlos has smuggled me in a burrito, which after a week of hospital food is like manna from heaven. Kyle sits in the chair beside me, reading me yet another get well card someone has sent. Who knew I'd become so popular?

"I have to ask, how did you know to come get me?" I ask softly when Carlos leaves to get me a soda.

Kyle frowns. "I was at home working on my computer, when random words started popping up on my screen." He stops, looking away. "It was Logan, Zoe. He was saying Zoe, Tower, Now, over and over. Then help her, help her help her. I dropped everything and drove out."

He looks up. "And you think I'm crazy."

In the corner of the room, Logan grins. "You better let the poor guy off the hook or he's going to have himself committed."

I touch the side of his face with my non bandaged hand.

"You don't sound crazy." I take a deep breath, ignoring the pain in my chest. "Remember when you told me that you felt like Logan brought me to you, because he knew you needed me?"

He nods.

"Well, you were wrong. Logan led me to you, because he knew I needed you. I didn't really understand why at the time, but he came to me and he told me—he told me I needed to let you in." I feel the tear slip down my face.

Kyle smiles, kissing the tips of my fingers. "I told the police I was worried about you because we were supposed to meet up and you weren't answering my texts. I told them I went to The Tower because I knew that sometimes you'd go up there to think."

"Thanks for that."

He shrugs. "Thanks for saving my life."

"Right back at you."

I yawn and he sits back. "Okay, you need some rest. The doc is thinking about releasing you tomorrow, so no funny business."

I grin and let his hand slip from mine. He kisses me on the forehead and leaves. As soon as he's gone Logan takes his place. I just let my head lull to the side, staring at him. His eyes are so green today, like emeralds. I want to burn the picture of his face into my mind. I want to be able to close my eyes any time I want and be able to see those eyes perfectly in my mind.

"He's right bruiser. You need to rest."

I chuckle. "I'll rest when I'm dead."

He frowns.

"What?" I ask, "Too soon?"

"I thought you were going to die. You almost did, Zoe."

A million responses go through my mind, the first of which is, would that really have been so terrible? But I don't say it out loud, because I know what his answer will be.

And, I know the truth. The truth is, hanging there, on that bridge, I could have let go. It would have been so easy to just not fight. But I couldn't. Something inside me, something I didn't even know existed, wanted to cling to life, to fight for it at any cost. It was that instinct that let me pull myself up, that surge of adrenaline that let me take down Mr. Mason. I guess I can't deny it any longer. The funny thing is that Logan saw it, even when I didn't.

"Well, I did promise." I say finally.

My first day back at school was like coming back from the dead. You'd have thought I was gone for three months instead of two weeks. Everyone hovers around me, alternately trying to get details on what happened and trying to play nurse. I let it go for a while, but by lunch I've had it. Madison is cutting my pizza into little squares so I can eat it with a fork, since my right arm is still in a sling.

"Okay, I'm hurt, but not an invalid. Knock it off." I say grumpily. She slides the plate back to me with a pout on her lips. "Sorry Madison. This is just a little too much smothering. But I really appreciate you trying to take care of me," I add quickly.

"Yeah, she's a tough cookie," Becker says, tossing a French fry at me. I can't help but grin.

"So, the voting for Homecoming Court is today. Have you voted yet? I can do it for you if you are too hurt to check the little boxes yourself," Darla offers playfully.

I nod.

"Yeah, I voted for Becker and Cassidy," I say pointing at them with my fork.

Cassidy puts her hand to her chest like I've just done something truly touching. Kyle leans over and whispers, "Kaylee always made everyone vote for her, no matter what."

I sigh. Kaylee was a bitch, even being dead couldn't elevate her to sainthood. My pity at the way she died only goes so far, and apparently, this is where that well runs dry. But I don't say anything, I just smile warmly.

"Cassidy would make a beautiful Homecoming Queen. I know, I've seen the dress."

"Which reminds me, what time do you want the limo to pick you up?" Becca asks, stabbing a bite of salad and stuffing it into her mouth.

"Limo? I thought that was a prom thing?"

She rolls her eyes, going for a piece of my cut pizza with her fork. I slide it away with a grin. "Normally, yes. But in light of everything, I've decided to pull out all the stops. Life is short right?"

Around the table people stare at her like she's said something wrong. I hold up my pizza so I can take a bite.

"Right."

In the corner booth Logan stares out the window at the people walking by.

The rest of the day goes by quickly, considering its Friday, and Homecoming. The halls are decorated in maroon and white streamers and posters plaster every wall. The dance is tonight, the game tomorrow. Kyle is a bundle of nerves.

"I'm still not back to one hundred per cent," he grumbles, rubbing his ribs gently. "And this is our toughest matchup this year."

Reaching up on my toes I kiss him softly, pressing out foreheads together. "I know. I'm so sorry you got hurt because of me."

He tilts my chin up. "Hey, it was worth it."

"Even if you lose tomorrow?"

He tilts his head back and forth like he's debating. Then he grins, "Yeah, even if."

I smile. "Good. Because, there's something I have

to take care of before the dance tonight, is it cool if I just meet you there?"

He looks puzzled. "Yeah, that's fine. But Madison will be very disappointed."

I frown, "I know. But she'll live and it's important."

Then, just as we are walking out of the front doors Becca comes running up to me, spinning me to face her.

"Hey Zoe, before you go, I want to show you something."

"Okay." I let her lead me back down the hall. "I'll see you tonight," I call out to Kyle, who waves goodbye.

Becca steers me toward one of the empty classrooms. Just when I'm sure something terrible is about to happen, all the girls yell, "Surprise!"

Becca claps. There's a tiny, one person size cake on the table. It says, *congratulations* in pink and green frosting.

"What's this about?"

She hugs me gently, careful to avoid the sling.

"You won Homecoming Queen, silly," Madison says, hugging me next. Cassidy is next in line.

"We all voted for you. And so did, like everyone else."

Wow. I'm so shocked I don't know what to say. Looking at their happy faces I'm completely speechless.

Becca laughs, "And that's why we decided to tell you now. Because it's customary for The Queen to give a short speech. We figured you'd need a little advance notice to gather your thoughts."

"I can't even…I don't know…thank you guys. So much." I feel like I'm going to cry as they collapse on me, in one big, group hug.

"You deserve it," Logan whispers over my shoulder.

Twenty-Five

I LET MOM SNAP A COUPLE PICTURES OF ME in my dress before I run out the door. Logan slips into the car with me.

"I appreciate you wanting me to be there, Zoe, but I'd really rather sit this one out," he says sadly.

"Oh, we aren't going to the dance."

He perks up in alarm. "Then where are we going?"

"You'll see."

I drive for about fifteen minutes, pulling into the cemetery parking lot.

"What are we doing here?" he asks as I get out of the car, careful not to catch my dress in the door.

"Just come on, there's someone I want you to meet."

I probably look hilarious climbing the stone wall in my tight lace dress, heels in hand, but I don't really care. I drop down on the other side, motioning for Logan to follow me. The moon is full and it sets the cemetery aglow with a soft white light. I come to a stop in a familiar part of the cemetery, not far from where Logan is buried. Kneeling in the soft grass I touch the white headstone, letting my fingers trace the name.

Thomas Parker Reed.

Beloved husband and father.

"Did I ever tell you how he died?"

Logan stands behind me, I can feel him like an extension of myself. Standing up, I close my eyes, picturing him in my mind. When I open them, The Reaper is standing between me and the headstone.

"Zoe," Logan reaches out but I wave him off.

"No, it's alright," I say softly. "I was sick. Stomach flu or something. I wanted some soup, but we didn't have any in the house. Dad was driving to the store to get some when he was hit by a drunk driver. He died and the other guy walked away without a scratch."

I take a deep breath. "I remember the police coming to the door that night. I saw my mom crumple to the floor like she was melting. And she looked over at me, this terrible look in her eyes, and I knew. It was my fault. He wouldn't have been on the road that night if it wasn't for me."

I feel Logan's hand wrap around my arm. "Zoe, it wasn't your fault."

I tilt my head. "I know. But I couldn't let it go, you know? I take a step forward and The Reaper holds out its hand to me. I take it, and it's as solid as Logan's.

The Reaper draws back its hood and my father's face is exposed to the moonlight. Throwing myself into his arms I let the tears flow freely, sniffling as I rub my face into his chest.

"Sweetheart. I'm so sorry." He strokes my hair, clutching me to him. "I never wanted to leave you, you know that."

I nod and sniffle again. "I know, daddy."

He pulls me back just a little, just enough so I can look up and see the pain in his eyes.

"You know what you have to do now?"

I shake my head. "I don't want to."

"Mr. Reed," Logan says breathlessly. "Zoe, how long have you known?"

"Since the bridge. It reached out to help me. I remember when I was little and I'd fall down, dad reaching down to help me up. I wasn't sure then. But later, in the hospital, I had a lot of time to think about it, to put the pieces together."

"My sweet, strong, stubborn little girl. Who else could it be? Who else could love so deeply and with so much courage that it could do all this? I'm so proud of you."

I drop his hand and turn to Logan. "I'm so sorry Logan, I didn't realize. He tried to tell me, even you knew on some level."

"What are you talking about Zoe? You aren't making any sense."

"It's me. It was never your unfinished business holding you here. It was always just me. And the more I needed you to be here, the stronger you became. That's why you were solid sometimes. It was because I needed you to be real so desperately, that I made you stay. I'm so, so sorry Logan."

"I don't understand," he says, taking my hands in his. "What does this mean?"

"It means that Zoe is a force of nature, a power all her own. She reached out and held on to us so tightly that we couldn't go, even when we were supposed to."

"I didn't mean to," I whisper. "I just couldn't lose you. Either of you."

Logan reaches out, touching the side of my face with the tips of his fingers.

"I know that, Zoe. I don't blame you. I didn't want to go either."

A tear rolls across my lip and into my mouth as I take a deep breath. "But now I have to do the hardest thing I've ever done, now I have to let you go."

He pulls me against him, and I can feel him, the full length of him from head to toe.

"No, you don't Zoe. Please," he begs.

In a heartbeat he's kissing me, deeply, desperately, like a dying man gasping for breath. His fingers are curled into my hair, clutching me to him. I break the kiss, pulling away just a little. I can taste the salty tears in my mouth.

"You can't stay. As much as you want to, as much as I want you to. You can't keep suffering like this."

He takes my face in his hands. "I would rather suffer for a million years and get to be close to you, than to lose you now. It's not fair. We only just found each other."

Hot tears stream down my face, rolling onto his hands.

It's my father's voice behind me that makes him look away.

"You won't be leaving her, not really. Time is different for us, Logan. A lifetime for her is only minutes where we're going. And you'll see her again."

He shakes his head. "How can you be so sure?"

"Because love, true love, is eternal. It's a bond that nothing can break. That's why you were given this time together. Your life was cut short, but this bond needed to be made before you could pass over, before she could release you."

I close my eyes, squeezing the remaining moisture from my eyes.

"I love you, Logan. I will love you forever. But we have to let each other go for now." The words are a knife in my heart. Nothing has ever been more painful than this, and if I live a hundred years, nothing ever will be.

"I love you too, Zoe." He kisses me again, this time it's a soft, gentle kiss, a kiss full of hope and promises unspoken. He releases me and steps back. "I'll be waiting for you."

"I know," I say, licking the last taste of him from my lips.

My father holds out his arm, leading Logan away from me. I feel a shudder start in the heels of my feet and quake its way up my body. He turns back, grinning over his shoulder.

"Do me a favor. Make me wait a really, really long time, okay?"

I nod because I don't dare open my mouth, I'm too afraid of what will come out. Tilting my head up to the sky I close my eyes, just breathing in and out slowly, trying to calm my shaking. When I open my eyes again they are both gone. I fall to my knees in the grass and sob into my hands. I don't know how long I cry, but I cry until the tears have run dry and I can't feel anything but the vast emptiness where Logan used to be. Crawling to my feet I dust myself off. I have a life to get back to. And I'd better make it a damn good one, because I'm not just living it for me. Not anymore.

Epilogue

THERE'S NO MUSIC IN THE ELEVATOR, making the ride feel like it's taking forever. Only Carlos and I are riding this trip. He's clutching my hand so tightly I think he might leave bruises. When the doors finally open a breeze blows my dress around mercilessly. My skin erupts in goosebumps, but I don't care. We walk slowly through the maze of ropes and out onto the observation deck. I don't even mind when the wind whips my carefully curled hair into a tangled mess. I walk to the edge, looking out across the vast horizon. Around me people are staring, but I don't care. Closing my eyes I take a deep breath, the scent of the east river hangs heavy in the air, filling my nostrils. The wind is cold as it blows the soft white fabric of my dress around my legs.

"I'm going to have to fix your hair in the cab," Carlos grumbles, pulling the black jacket tight around him with a shiver.

"I just need a minute alone," I say, my words carried away in the morning air.

He nods, "I'll be inside."

I cling to the edge of the green metal railing, pressing my face against the mesh. The other people spread out, giving me space. I take another deep breath.

"I can't believe it's been five years since you left," I whisper, letting the wind carry the words away. "I miss you every day."

My heart aches in my chest and I fight it back because, today of all days, I have to hold myself together.

"I just wanted to come here and tell you, I'm happy. But you probably know that. I'm sure you're up there somewhere stalking me like always." I bite my bottom lip, chewing off the lipstick I'd so carefully applied this morning. "But mostly, I just want to say, thank you. And…I love you."

The wind picks up and I feel the chill run along my skin, comforting and cold. A caress I haven't felt in a very long time.

Carlos peeks his head out the door. "Seriously Zoe, you're going to be late for your own wedding. You don't want to keep Kyle waiting."

I sigh, smiling into the wind and wiping the hair out of my eyes. The truth is, Kyle would wait for me forever. Over the years he's been the one constant in my life, the one thing I've never had to doubt. He's the person I want to spend the rest of my life with--the person I love most in the world. I only came here because I couldn't think of any better way to get Logan's attention. Even though I haven't seen him since the night he finally crossed over, I still feel him sometimes. I felt him the day I graduated high school, the day I stood on a volcano in Hawaii, and most recently, the night Kyle proposed. And I feel him with me today.

I touch the bodice of my white dress, where the old bottle cap sits on a chain next to my heart. "Well come on then. Let's not make him wait anymore."

Acknowledgements

First and always foremost I need to thank my family for their patience, love, and support. My husband Jeremy and my original trilogy, Jonathan, Sidney, and Camille, you guys are the center of my world—even when I'm locked in the office for days at a time. I love you more than you will ever know.

I would also like to send big thanks and love to my extended family, my parents by blood, and by marriage, and the siblings I never had but always wanted, and my crazy cousins. You guys are beyond compare and I thank God every day that I get to be part of your lives.

When it comes down to publishing a book, there is always a fear that I imagine is similar to walking a tight rope without a net. Fear of failure, fear of ridicule, and top of my list, fear that you are wasting your time with something that will never see the light of day. Writing this book was one of the biggest risks I've ever taken, not because I didn't love the story but because I was being told that publishers would never buy it and people never read it. It was too 'paranormal' or too 'off trend'. But I loved Zoe and Logan and so I stuck my head in the sand and did it anyway. And I'm really glad I did.

It's on that note that I want to thank my publishing family for catching me when I decided to let go. The folks at Clean Teen Publishing—Courtney, Dyan, Marya, and Rebecca—you ladies have been a joy and a blast to work for. I have never had such a good time publishing a book before. YOU make this look easy. (And big hugs and thanks to Angie Townsend for introducing us and encouraging me to submit to them.)

Thanks to everyone who helped me in the filming of the Losing Logan Book trailer, Monica, Kaydie, Krystie, Cody, and of course, everyone who came out to be an extra or just an extra hand. You guys are amazing!

I would be remiss if I didn't mention my biggest fan, cheerleader, tech support, and life coach Danette Westerfield. A brilliant author in her own right, she still manages to make time for me and I could never repay her kindness and love.

Special thanks to my blogger friends, especially Kayleigh, Brooke, Dvora, Amber, Bev, and Colette. Without dedicated book lovers like you, our books would just linger in the void of obscurity, so thank you deeply for all you do.

I would also like to give a big shout out to my Minion Army! There's far too many of you to list here, but please know that I love and appreciate each and every one of you!

And last but never least; I would like to thank you, dear reader. You have trusted me to take you on a journey and I sincerely hope you have enjoyed the ride. Without YOU, none of the rest matters.

A quick note about the dedication

I debated for a long time about this but I thought it was funny, so I kept it. But at the end of the day, there's nothing funny about bullying. Yes, it happens to all of us at some point, but that doesn't make it okay. If you are struggling, I can only say that you are not alone. There are people who love you and who want to help you and I sincerely hope you will seek them out.

And should you find yourself on the opposite side of that coin, you are not alone either. We have all, at some point, been cruel to someone whether on purpose or without thinking, but what matters—what makes you the person you will become—is what you do to make it right.

We are all flawed. If we can see beauty in those flaws and offer kindness instead of criticism, the world will be a much better place. And that begins with you.

Love,
Sherry

About the Author

Sherry D. Ficklin is a full time writer from Colorado where she lives with her husband, four kids, two dogs, and a fluctuating number of chickens and house guests. A former military brat, she loves to travel and meet new people. She can often be found browsing her local bookstore with a large white hot chocolate in one hand and a towering stack of books in the other. That is, unless she's on deadline at which time she, like the Loch Ness monster, is only seen in blurry photographs.

She is the author of The Gods of Fate Trilogy

now available from Dragonfly Publishing. Her previously self-published novel After Burn: Military Brats has been acquired by Harlequin and will be released in 2014 with a second book in that series to follow. Her newest YA steampunk novel, Extracted: The Lost Imperials book 1, co-written with Tyler H. Jolley is now available everywhere books are sold and her newest YA novel, Losing Logan, is due for release in 2014 from Clean Teen Publishing.

CPSIA information can be obtained at www.ICGtesting.com
Printed in the USA
LVOW10s2017030914

402280LV00003B/140/P